Die Before "I Do"

A Simone Simpson Mystery

Rita Smircich

Die Before "I Do"

A Simone Simpson Mystery

Rita Smircich

Published by "I Do" LLC

Cover design by Chris Murphy: www.cmurph.com
Book design by Pamela Pitcher: pam@documentclarity.com

Paperback ISBN: 978-1-7335014-0-8
Second Edition

Printed in the United States of America 2021

Special thanks to Judith Marks-White, whose encouragement helped me find my literary voice. Her patience, teachings and friendship are the building blocks to this book.

Thank you to my family and friends who believed in me, and have encouraged me to, "Stop talking about it - write it!"

Dedication:
*There are times when unexpected moments occur. Some are
once-in-a-lifetime events that can be positive, negative, painful,
uplifting, and even life-altering. And then, without warning or
explanation, suddenly there is a premonition that something
wonderfully unforeseen is about to happen. For me, it came by way
of a man named Ed, who took the ordinary and made it extraordinary.
It is to him, with gratitude and love, I dedicate this book.*

CHAPTER 1

The taxi sat at a red light on Eighth Street and McDougal in New York City's Greenwich Village. From the backseat, Simone's eyes darted from one side of the street to the other, taking in her eclectic surroundings, feeling like a young child in a candy store, not knowing which jar of gems to look at first. A pan handler begged for change from a passerby, homeless men slept in a fetal position in a doorway, and a squeegee man washed car windows.

Her gaze locked on the dirty windows of a store with haphazardly taped placards of *Peace Is the Answer,* and, *Make Love - Not War.* To the right of the entrance was an oversized poster: *FEAR - Forget Everything And Run, or Face Everything And Rise, The Choice is Yours.*

Finally, Simone arrived at her dorm room at New York University, feeling anxious. She placed her mod podge valise at her heels and inspected the modestly furnished room. A twin bed was nestled under the only window in the room. Snuggled against the white pillow was a beloved stuffed brown bear, missing a black button eye. The walls were whitewashed a dull yellow, speckled with rectangles of sticky tape stains that once secured posters of the previous occupant's adored rock bands. Or perhaps, photos of anorexic fashion models that reminded the young impressionable teens of their questionable self-esteem.

She stood alone in the room, but only a few feet away on the other side of the brick wall, was the fast-paced cornucopia of diverse cultures. She watched people of different colors, dress, and ages walk past the bedroom window. Would she fit into this collegial tapestry, she wondered.

Fear stirred. She could feel her undigested food turning, her heart racing, and moisture evaporating from her mouth. Simone's thoughts floated to the FEAR poster she had seen moments before. If she allowed her own fear to take control and she ran back home to Louisville, she would never leave again, destined to live the life as a spinster in her parents' home, and eventually become their caretaker. Or, she could face this adventure; embrace it with courage and determination. The consequence being: she could never go home again.

All her life, Simone Deschamps wanted to get away from her father's physical abuse, and hoped to attend New York University. They fought frequently about the subject, with Simone losing the battle, but gaining new bruises. He had a good paying job, so her parents could afford to send her to NYU, but he insisted she attend a local community college and live at home. Both her parents went to college and got jobs they loved, so why wouldn't he allow Simone to do the same? Was she not good enough to follow her dream? She was determined, bucked his abuse, and forged ahead. She applied to NYU, was accepted, and was offered a full scholarship. Much to her father's objection, she accepted the university's offer. She finally felt free. And fear.

In the hallway she heard the enthusiastic voices of parents assisting their children with their belongings. Simone had no boxes, no posters, and no one to hug her good bye. "If you leave this house, young lady, you can never come back," her father's voice echoed in her head. Her anxiety morphed into a wave of confidence and strength, Reminiscent of the poster, Simone repeated her new mantra, "Face Everything And Rise." The door opened, and standing there was a teenaged girl, equally wide-eyed and looking just as apprehensive as Simone. Behind her stood the girl's parents. Simone's face involuntarily turned into a smile when she heard the woman speak in a familiar southern accent, "Hi, we're Virginia and Henry Smith. And this is our daughter, Judy."

"Hello," the young girl announced.

"Hi, I'm Simone."

Judy's parents shook hands with Simone, which broke the growing silence in the room.

"I hope you don't mind, I took the bed by the window," said Judy.

"No, not at all."

The two girls shared a lack of life experiences outside of their southern homes. Their similarities and sense of adventure drew them together.

They became fast friends, watching out for each other while they explored the university, and the sights of New York City.

Simone wrote a letter to her parents every week. She expressed her excitement about attending NYU, life in Manhattan, and about Judy, explaining that she, too, was from the south. With her letters she included photographs of the campus, her dorm room, and of the two girls standing in front of prominent landmarks. She had hoped that her father would accept her happiness, and forgive her for moving thousands of miles away. Despite the pain she had endured by his hand, she still craved his love.

She never received a letter back from them, or from her brother to whom she also wrote. She telephoned her parents a few times, but when her father answered, he would immediately hang up when he heard, "Papa." When she tried calling back the line would be busy for hours.

Judy's parents, aware of Simone's abandonment, invited her to join them at their home in Virginia for the holidays.

"Simone," Mrs. Smith said one afternoon over lunch, "Judy told us that you don't have a place to stay during the summer. Would you like to stay with us until the next semester begins in September?"

"Oh, thank you so much, Mrs. Smith," Simone gushed. "I'd love that." The two girls, overcome with excitement, hugged each other.

Simone's heart surged with happiness. But through the waves of love bestowed on Simone, she couldn't help feel a bit envious of Judy for the life she lived. Mr. Smith was kind and he treated his wife and daughter with respect. Mrs. Smith was a strong woman with an abundance of love to give everyone who crossed her path.

"I really wish you would call me Virginia, and my husband, Henry. Folks around here call me Virginia from Virginia."

"Oh no. I could never do that," Simone said. "I was raised not to call my elders by their first names. Not that you and Mr. Smith are old," Simone interjected quickly.

By the end of the semester, Simone moved all of her neatly packed possessions into the Smith's garage, a tradition that followed for the next three years.

CHAPTER 2

Over the next two years, Simone's fears of living in New York City dissipated. She reached out to freshmen, helped them navigate the transportation system, the campus grounds, and occasionally tutored in French. She had become a thread in the New York City tapestry.

She got a part time job at a local eatery, but quit after a month as the bus boy, the owner's son, stole her tips off the tables. The wages were meager, and she didn't think it was worth fighting. She left, and got a part time job in the school's library. When she lived in Kentucky, she worked in the local library after school. Here, she was in a comfortable surrounding where she could browse books about foreign lands, and fantasize about future adventures.

For seven months, Simone dutch-dated Jeff, a fellow student. They split all expenses, often making Simone feel Jeff was more of a pal to hang around with, than a boyfriend. He never offered to pay, and she wondered if this was the norm in New York City.

"He's never offered to treat?" Judy asked.

"Not once. Not even on our first date."

She and Judy double dated a few times. Each time, Jeff asked Simone to give him money ahead of time, so that when the bill was presented, Jeff appeared to be paying for Simone.

Judy expressed her dismay to her roommate. "You know, the other guys aren't going to ask you out if they see you with Jeff all the time. Maybe they think he's your steady boyfriend. Who knows what he's telling his buddies."

This made Simone think about her relationship with Jeff – or lack of one. Most weekends they spent walking around the East Village, watching the diverse crowds at Washington Square Park, or they went to a movie, followed by burgers at Phebe's on Fourth Street. Simone got bored with this routine, and eventually with Jeff, and his cheapness. He reminded her of her father, and of her brother.

Simone talked to the college's social worker about her willingness to accept the way Jeff had treated her, and she realized that Jeff's behavior was another form of abuse. The social worker gave Simone solid advice: No one can abuse you, unless you allow them to.

A week later, when she and Judy left to go to the Smith's home for the summer, Simone parted ways with Jeff. Surprisingly, she found it easy to walk away from him, without any tears or drama.

Through the months, Simone longed to speak to her mama, but phone calls and letters were never answered. Despite the silence, she continued to send a letter home frequently, and each week her mailbox continued to be empty. Except, one day in January of her junior year, she received the following:

Dearest Simone,

I love you and I miss you so much. But you can never come home again, call, or write. Your Papa has forbidden it because you disobeyed him. I'm sending this letter from Mrs. Genet's home; I help her now with shopping as she is getting too old to go to the market.

As soon as Papa sees a letter from you, he tears it up and puts it in the trashcan. He caught me taking your letter from the garbage, and, as a result, I spent two days in hospital because of a broken arm. I told the doctor I fell down the stairs, tripping over my nightgown.

Your Papa is drinking much more these days. He stopped going to Cleary's because he has gotten tickets for driving drunk. He stays home, drinking, watching my every move. His anger is quick to surface. So please, my beautiful daughter, do not send any more letters to our home. Do not call. I fear your Papa will not stop at a broken arm.

My heart aches for you, to see your beautiful face, to hear your voice, to hold you in my arms like I did when you were a child. I pray for you every night, and ask God to watch over you and to protect you.

I love you very much, Mama

Simone sent back a response to her mother at Mrs. Genet's address. Secret and sacred letters were exchanged weekly. Her heart soured

with delight knowing her mother was back in her life. Her mother understood the risk, but was willing to take it.

Then, four months later, Simone received a registered letter:

Dear Simone.

*I'm sorry to tell you that your parents were killed this past Friday night
in a deadly collision on their way home from dinner. The car left the
road, and it smashed into a large tree. The police said your father was
driving drunk. They both died instantly.*

*I hope you will be able to come home to say goodbye to them. I have
tried to contact your brother, but he does not return my calls. Your parents will be held at the Greene Funeral Home in town, until you or Jean-
Paul come to claim their bodies.*

I am deeply sorry to give you this terrible news. May God bless you.

Mrs. Mary Genet

Simone threw herself on her bed and cried for hours. She would
never again see or hug her Mama. As for Papa, he had died in her heart
ages ago. There would never be a time for reconciliation.

How was she going to come up with the money to fly home and say
goodbye? Her funds were dwindling, and what she had left was needed
to get her through until she could get a summer job. She didn't want to
ask Judy's parents for money. They had already done so much for her.

She lifted the dormitory phone and asked to be connected to Mr.
Jean-Paul Deschamps in Kentucky. It was apparent to Simone, since
Jean-Paul didn't answer any of her letters that he wouldn't want anything
to do with her. She was convinced her brother was more like her father –
mean, cheap and unforgiving.

After a few minutes, he answered the phone.

"Jean-Paul, hi, it's Simone."

"Who?"

"Jean-Paul, don't be mean. It's your sister. I didn't call to argue. I
called to tell you I received a registered letter from Mrs. Genet saying our
parents were killed in a car accident. . ."

"Yes, the police already contacted me," he answered, cutting his
sister off. "I've gone to the funeral home and made burial plans."

Simone was shocked, "Why didn't you call me?"

"I don't know where you are. Papa told me he hasn't heard from you since you moved to New York three years ago."

"That's a lie!" Simone cried into the phone. "I wrote to them every week, but they never responded. I was told not to return home. I never meant to hurt them," Simone sobbed. "They wanted me to stay home, so I could take care of them in their declining years."

Changing the subject, he asked, "How did Mrs. Genet know your address?"

"I assume Mama had given it to her." She kept the exchange of letters a secret.

"That meddling old biddy," Jean-Paul said with disgust. "I bet she's telling all the neighbors that Papa was a drunk."

"I doubt she would say anything. She is a very sweet lady." Their father's drinking wasn't a neighborhood secret. Many saw him staggering home, but she didn't add this to the conversation.

"So why are you calling me? Don't tell me that now you want to come home and cry on their bodies and ask for forgiveness?"

Simone was silent for a moment, inhaling deep breaths. Steadily, and without emotion, she said, "I don't have any money to fly home, so I won't be able to make it to their funeral. Can you forgive me?"

Now it was Jean-Paul's turn to be silent.

"Jean-Paul, are you still there?"

"Yes, I'm thinking."

After another long silence, he continued, "Alright," he acquiesced, "I'll wire you some money. Although Papa abandoned you, he didn't legally disown you. You are entitled to half their money. Whatever is in their estate, I'll share with you, less the money I'm sending you to return home for their funeral. You should be there to say good-bye to Mama."

She was stunned. "Thank you Jean-Paul. I'm looking forward . . ." But he hung up before she could finish the sentence.

Simone received the wired funds that day, and two days later she was back in Kentucky. She stayed in her old bedroom, wandering around the house as if seeing it for the first time. Recollection of arguments, beatings, and the terror her father evoked flashed through her mind. She couldn't wait to remove the dust-tinged memories and return to New York, where she was living a new and healthier life.

Attendance at the funeral parlor was meager. No one from their family came to pay their respects except for Aunt Agnes, her mother's sister, who, like Jean-Paul, traveled back to their respective homes at the end of the evening. Her aunt apologized for not wanting to stay with Simone, but she would not consider staying where so many horrors had occurred.

Mrs. Genet came to the funeral home, holding onto the arm of her grown son. She embraced Simone and cried on the passing of her parents. She nodded to Jean-Paul, said a polite 'hello' but did not extend any condolences to him.

Jean-Paul's wife and twin daughters did not come to the funeral, saying the babies were too young. He never extended an invitation to his sister to stay with his family after the funeral. Simone wondered if he abused his wife, too, keeping her away from the eyes of others, the same way Papa did to Mama.

As Executor to their parent's will, Jean-Paul made all the funeral arrangements, and would take care of all the legal issues. He promised Simone he would share any monies from life insurance policies, investments, and the eventual sale of the house.

By the following Sunday, Simone was back in her dorm room studying for finals. Virginia and Henry Smith had again extended the invitation to spend the summer at their home in Charlottesville, where the two girls would return to their annual summer jobs as waitresses at the local country club. The year was bittersweet, as Simone knew that next year, after graduation, she would most likely stay in New York, get an apartment, and find a job.

Jean-Paul kept his word. Simone received a check for $28,000, her share of her parents' estate. Once the house sold, he would send her another check for half the proceeds.

Simone decided the inherited money was going to be saved for her future, but she wanted to spend some of it on a special treat. That evening while Mrs. Smith was preparing dinner, Simone asked, "May I have a private word with you?"

"Sure, honey. What's on your mind?"

"Mrs. Smith, if Judy is interested, would you let her travel to Paris for two weeks? I'm taking $5,000 of my parents' money to pay for the trip. I wanted to ask you privately because if you say no, I don't want Judy to be upset. It's my way of saying thank you to you and Judy for all you've done for me these past years."

"What a very generous offer, Simone. Of course I will need to speak to Mr. Smith about this idea. It's extremely gracious of you to ask us first. Have you ever traveled in Europe before?"

"No. I've never been past Kentucky until coming to New York. I'd like to see Paris, and I would feel better having Judy with me. My father was born in France and insisted we only speak French at home. I also tutored during my high school years, and at NYU. Maybe I'll find some relatives there, as I no longer have anyone to call family." Simone burst into tears.

Virginia pulled the young woman gently into her arms. Simone's body shook against Mrs. Smith as her tears fell.

She cried for the pain inflicted by her father and her inability to stop the abuse, and his drunkenness that caused their deaths. Most of all, she cried for the loss of her mother's embrace.

CHAPTER 3

Later, while getting ready for bed, Virginia expressed her concern to her husband. "Henry, do you think the girls will be safe in Paris? They are young, and it will be the first time they're traveling alone."

"I'm sure they'll be," answered Henry. Reassuring his wife, he added, "I'll make some phone calls in the morning, and see if we can get the girls to stay at the apartment on Rue des Barres. They'll have to pay for housekeeping, but it'll be cheaper than staying in a hotel."

Henry thought for a moment, then said, "I'll talk to Cathy in my office. Her sister lives in the outskirts of Paris. I'm sure she has a housekeeper who can open up the apartment, freshen it up, stock it with essentials, and keep an eye on them. I'm sure the girls will be fine."

"Our little girl is growing up so quickly, Henry. Soon, we'll be empty nesters," Virginia lamented.

"We knew the day would come sooner or later. I need to get to sleep. I have a big case in the morning."

It was late June, and Paris smelled of lavender.

The girls made their way to the apartment at Rue des Barres, a block from the Seine. They were greeted by the doorman, who welcomed them and provided a key to the Penthouse apartment.

"Wow, Judy," exclaimed Simone. "This apartment is beautiful. How did your father arrange this?"

"Someone in his office owns it, and told my dad, anytime he wants to use it, he can. There's also a housekeeper that comes with the apartment," added Judy.

The apartment had three oversized bedrooms, each with their own private bathroom. Fourteen foot ceilings were adorned with intricately carved crown molding. The walls were covered with wallpaper dating back to the 1940s. Pine floorboards smelling of polish ran throughout the apartment. Sunshine coming through large, double hung windows, filled the rooms with light and a view of the Seine. The overall apartment was furnished with antiques, many showing their age with scratches, chips and peeling varnish. But Simone didn't care – the apartment was beautiful.

A note, written in French, was left on the kitchen table informing the girls that basic essentials, such as cream, eggs and cheese were in the refrigerator. Bread, along with tins of food and pans were in the larder. Charlene wrote she'd be back in the morning to make their beds and provide fresh linens. She left her phone number in case the girls thought of something they needed or wanted.

"I might never want to go home," exclaimed Simone. "I love this apartment, the location . . . I love Paris!"

"Let's go sightseeing," said Judy. "I don't want to waste any time being inside."

The girls stood in front of the mighty cathedral of Notre-Dame de Paris, their eyes widened, gripped by the flying buttresses, the stained glass windows, and its overall architecture. Postcards and photographs could not capture the cathedral's splendor. Simone wondered why her father, who was an architect born and raised in France, never took them to Paris. So many things her father did made her question his motivations.

Simone, missing her mother, cried as she knelt before the statue of the Madonna surrounded by flickering devotion candles. Yet, ironically, it was her death which ultimately allowed Simone to see Paris.

Judy, sensing Simone's sadness kneeled alongside her, extending an arm around her friend's shoulders. The two women, bonded as eternal friends, were at the end of their two week Parisian adventure. Tomorrow they were scheduled to fly back to the States and on to the Smith's home, before returning to NYU for their senior year.

Simone fell in love with Paris, with the rich culture, the delectable food, and the intricate architecture.

And she fell in love with Joe Simpson.

Chapter 4

Their last night in Paris, Simone and Judy went to a local restaurant for a late night supper. The bistro was filled with locals dancing and singing to lively music.

Seated at the table next to them was a man dining alone. The three struck up a conversation. He introduced himself as Joe Simpson, a hedge fund trader in New York, traveling on business. There was something about Joe that fascinated Simone, and she felt an immediate attraction. His blue eyes drew her in and his smile was honest. He wasn't flashy, just an attractive, down-to-earth guy. She whispered to Judy, "He seems nice."

He asked Simone to dance. Her immediate reaction was to shake her head, no. Then she looked at Judy who waved her hand, "I'll be fine. Go . . . go."

While they danced to the French chanson music, his arms circled around her waist, molding them perfectly together. Simone felt comfortable. She didn't feel the need to pull back, or feel threatened, as she would when her father grabbed her. Instead, she allowed herself to relax and enjoy being held.

Joe asked for her phone number, promising to call once he got back to New York. She gave him the Smith's number, stressing she would only be there for another three weeks, before returning to NYU. Given the logistical roadblocks, she thought she would never hear from him again, that this was merely a nice guy showing her a good time before leaving Paris.

Joe was enthralled with Simone. And he did call, two days before she and Judy were to leave Virginia for New York. She felt giddy hearing his voice. They arranged a date for a Saturday in mid-September.

Joe took Simone to see the ballet, "Romeo and Juliet," at Lincoln Center. Although Simone explored many areas of the city, the ballet was beyond her limited budget. She was enthralled by the beauty of the venue, the performance, but mostly by Joe and his ability to make her feel comfortable and safe.

They had dinner afterwards at Chez Louisette, a quaint French restaurant near Lincoln Center. Simone ordered Sole Meunière, fork tender Dover Sole accented with silky brown butter and fresh lemon juice. Joe ordered a hearty Boeuf Bourguignon, simmered for hours in lardons, root vegetables and a hint of minty thyme. They ended their meal sharing a Pear Tarte Tatin and bold French roast coffee.

During dinner they reminisced about when they first met, and the beauty of Paris, the City of Lights and Love. Simone told him about her parents' recent deaths. Joe explained that his family lived in Pennsylvania, he was twenty-nine (older than she thought), and lives in an apartment in Tribeca.

From that night on, they became inseparable, spending all their free time together. When Simone wasn't with Joe, she was in school. She left her job at the library and took a part-time job as assistant to a well-established wedding planner. She loved the job and enjoyed the fast pace. Every wedding presented something new and exciting. And the pay was triple what she made at the library.

In early December, weeks before Simone and Judy were to leave for Charlottesville for winter break, Joe and Simone met again at Chez Louisette.

They danced, laughed, dined, and drank expensive champagne.

Joe whispered, "Simone, we've only known each other for six months, but I've fallen in love with you."

"Joe, I care about you very much, but we really don't know each other very long."

"I'm sorry if I'm being too pushy. I know what I want when I see it. And you're it. Take all the time you need, but know what I'm feeling."

Joe returned Simone to her dorm at NYU where they kissed under the glow of the city streetlight.

He suggested, "Perhaps during the Christmas holiday you can come to Philadelphia and meet my folks. We'll return to New York, and spend New Year's Eve together."

"Joe, that sounds wonderful. I'll talk to Judy and her parents. I'm sure it'll be ok."

"I'll miss you, Simone."

"And I'll miss you."

Chapter 5

The day after Christmas, Simone took the train from Virginia to Philadelphia. Joe met her at the station and brought her to meet his parents and siblings. Waves of confusion ensued.

"Joe has told us all about you," said his father. "But he didn't tell us how beautiful you are." She was introduced to his brothers, their wives and children, a few aunts, uncles and cousins. She was overwhelmed, but felt welcomed.

Then, the inevitable happened. His mother said, "Let me show you to your room. Unless you plan on sleeping with my son under my roof?"

Silence blanketed the room, interspersed with whispering mumbles from Joe about such an inappropriate question.

"My own room, please," Simone answered quickly. Joe did say his mother was overprotective, but she seemed more passive aggressive and rude.

"Right this way," Mrs. Simpson responded. She followed the woman upstairs to a sunny guest room. "Dinner is at 6:00. We dress for the occasion," she said looking her guest up and down.

Of course she had packed an appropriate outfit. Did Joe's mother think she was a country bumpkin? She wasn't sure how her relationship with Joe's mother was going work, or not. They certainly didn't get off on the right start.

The next morning, Joe and Simone returned to New York, and taxied to Joe's apartment in Tribeca. Around the room were five dozen long-stemmed roses, which Joe's assistant had purchased and had placed beforehand. Simone's eyes widened at the sight of the flowers, the large and well-appointed apartment, and the views of the city's skyline. When she turned back to look at Joe, he was on one knee, holding a two karat diamond engagement ring.

"Simone, I love you. Please be my wife."

Simone burst into tears, unable to control her emotions. "Yes, oh yes, Joe. I will marry you."

Joe's assistant had also accomplished one more task – food from Chez Louisette. On the sideboard was a buffet of food intended to be served at room temperature: an oversized butcher board of Charcuterie, with various cheeses, an assortment of cured meats, rich pâtés, cornichons, olives, bread and jams. Near the dining table was a metal ice bucket filled to capacity with a jumble of ice cubes that kept a bottle of Dom Perignon chilled. In the refrigerator was a large Nicoise Salad, and a platter of grilled salmon. Simone and Joe dined by candlelight amidst the intoxicating scent of roses.

After dinner, Joe prepared coffee. He removed delicate pots of Mousse au Chocolat from the refrigerator and placed them on the table. While the coffee dripped, Simone washed the dishes. Joe walked up behind her, and put his arms around her waist. "I love you Simone," he whispered into her ear.

A sudden shock ran through her, flashing her back to when she was sixteen. She recalled standing at the kitchen sink washing dishes after the family meal, as she was doing now, when her father walked up behind her and pressed his body up against hers. She could feel her father's erection, turning her stomach, almost causing her to retch her undigested dinner onto the dirty dishes. He whispered in her ear, "I need to talk to your mother about this slop she called dinner. If I hear one peep from you, you're next." Spittle from her father's mouth made its way into Simone's hair, leaving behind the smell of beer and tobacco, odors that lingered until the next morning. She knew what was next – her mother would suffer at the hands of the monster, the man she called her father – the man she hated with all her heart.

Simone's body tightened at the memory. Her father's wrath had risen from his grave, reigniting the fear she had so successfully buried with his body.

"Are you alright, Simone?" Joe asked.

She answered quickly, "Yes. I think it's all the excitement . . . the food . . . the ring . . . the flowers . . . I guess I just got a bit overwhelmed."

She could not tell Joe the horrors she and her mother had endured. Abused victims kept their secrets.

Chapter 6

Simone called Judy the next morning. "You won't believe what happened. Joe asked me to marry him, and I said yes."

"I'm so glad you said yes. I was hoping you would."

Taken aback with shock, Simone asked, "What do you mean?"

"Joe had asked my dad for your hand in marriage."

Simone was speechless . . . dazed. "He did what?"

"Yes. Apparently, he came down to our home a few weeks ago and met with my parents. He told them he wanted to marry you, but he wanted to ask my dad for your hand in marriage. They were so honored."

"Wow. I had no idea. So you knew all this time?" Simone was feeling a little bit upset that Judy knew before she had.

"Oh no. My parents didn't tell me until this morning, while we were having breakfast. They know me too well. I would have blabbed."

The two women laughed.

When's the wedding?"

"We're thinking right after graduation, and I'd love to have the ceremony and reception at the Boar's Head Inn in Charlottesville."

"That's a wonderful idea, Simone. I'm so happy for you."

Simone asked Judy to be her maid of honor, which she enthusiastically accepted.

"See you in a few days," they said in unison.

Simone hung up and looked at Joe. He was reading the newspaper and sipping coffee. She studied his face. This was a man of character, a man who would make a wonderful husband, she thought. If only I could tell Mama about him.

CHAPTER 7

Simone did her best not to be a difficult bride. As a part time wedding planner, she interacted with women who were unkind and demanding. Her goal was to enjoy every minute of their wedding day.

Joe's mother was cordial to Simone, giving her a tentative hug and an air-kiss. She and her husband did not contribute to the cost of the wedding. Although Joe's family was wealthy, Simone assumed they were not happy with his choice.

"Joe, I don't think your mother likes me," Simone mentioned a few months earlier.

Joe confessed, "She wanted me to marry a woman I dated several years ago. Our families were members of the same country club, and our parents were friends. Her father was my pediatrician. But, when it came down to it, I didn't love the woman. I love you, Simone, and that is all that matters."

"You look beautiful, Simone," Mr. Smith said, as he prepared to walk her down the aisle. "My wife and I are so honored to be celebrating this momentous occasion."

"Thank you for loving me like a daughter," she responded. "I couldn't ask for a more perfect role model."

"Simone, don't get me weepy before I hand you off to Joe," he said with a slight chuckle, trying not to break down into tears. "Now let's get you married, young lady."

Henry escorted Simone along the white runner, placed over the expansive manicured lawn. He lifted Simone's veil, gave her a kiss, and placed her hand in Joe's. "You take care of my little girl, young man."

"I will, sir. I promise."

Simone Marié Dechamps and Joseph Patrick Simpson exchanged their vows at the elegant Boar's Head Inn in Charlottesville, Virginia. They were surrounded by nature's bounty under an old Willow tree. In the background, peacocks serenaded with mating calls, and, as if on cue, Canada geese flew in formation honking their approval. A family of wood ducks marched across the lawn, adding to the attendees.

In addition to Joe's immediate family, and the Smiths, Mrs. Mary Genet, and Aunt Agnes came with their sons as escorts. Jean-Paul declined the invitation.

The couple spent two weeks on their honeymoon, staying in Oscar Wilde's 377 square foot room, #16, at L'Hôtel on the Left Bank of Paris. The room was well-appointed with period furniture and a private bathroom. Every morning on their terrace they enjoyed buttery, flakey, croissants and a variety of seasonal, home-made raspberry and apricot jams, washed down with roasted French coffee.

During the day, they explored Paris and enjoyed the city's sights and sounds. They took photos from the top of la tour Eiffel, walked for endless hours through the Louvre, and enjoyed a relaxing boat ride on the Seine. Every afternoon, they took a break from sight-seeing, and enjoyed people-watching at an outdoor café, evenings they indulged in a late supper of superlative French cuisine. Simone had never known such happiness or love.

She was finally free to let go of her past demons, and let herself love completely.

CHAPTER 8

Over the next three years, they discussed starting a family. Joe wanted to save money and buy a house in Westchester County, thinking the city wasn't the place to raise a family.

The week before Christmas, they planned to see The Nutcracker, followed by dinner at their favorite restaurant, Chez Louisette, which had now become a Christmas tradition. Over dinner she would tell Joe the good news: she was pregnant, the baby was due in July. They would tell Joe's family on Christmas Eve, and the Smith's on Christmas Day. Simone was glowing with happiness and anticipation.

When they left the ballet, there was a storm brewing, dropping snow combined with pelting rain that stung Simone's cheeks. They walked slowly and carefully to the restaurant, the streets and sidewalks becoming more slippery every minute. They snuggled next to each other, sharing an umbrella, and discussed the excitement of the ballet.

As they crossed the avenue, the tapping of icy rain on their umbrella was muted by the blaring sound of a car horn from a speeding taxicab, trying to beat the traffic light. The driver noticed Joe and Simone too late. He slammed on the brakes; the car slid sideways across the intersection. Joe's body took the brunt of the impact.

Simone dragged her body over to Joe's, screaming and crying as she held his head in her lap. Joe slowly looked at his wife, and before closing his eyes for the last time whispered, "I will always love you, Simone."

CHAPTER 9

Judy rushed to be at Simone's side, staying with her in the hospital while Simone recovered from surgery to repair a broken leg and arm. Sadly, she lost the baby, and never got to tell Joe he was to be a father. There weren't any surgical procedures, tinctures, medicinal pills or firewater to heal Simone's broken heart.

Simone was in a wheelchair for two weeks, and then on crutches for the following four weeks. Since her leg and arm were in a cast, Judy did everything for her. She bathed and dressed her, did all the shopping, cooking and cleaning. She answered phone calls, wrote letters and thank you notes. Sometimes she had to turn away friends and neighbors who meant well, but whose imposing questions upset Simone. There were times Judy had to force-feed Simone, who wanted to give up and stop living. But Judy persevered. She got her friend to smile. And then one day, over something funny that Judy had said, Simone laughed. It was a small step toward recovery.

Mrs. Smith came up from Virginia to take over, as Judy had to go back to work in Richmond. Mrs. Smith stayed with Simone for the next six weeks, helping her adjust to her new life, taking her to doctor's appointments and to physical therapy.

Mr. Smith, an attorney, stayed with his wife and Simone. He helped her go through legal documents, court papers and medical forms. They took Simone to meetings with her attorney and financial planner.

"I can't thank you and Judy enough for all you've done these past two months. I'm so grateful and lucky," Simone said. "To think, Joe survived 9-11 simply because he couldn't hail an available taxi that morning to get him to his office at the World Trade Center. And ironically, it was a taxi that took his life."

All the words of comfort and encouragement couldn't erase the pervasive memory of that horrific night.

Mrs. Smith called Jean-Paul to tell him about Joe's death and of Simone's condition. His wife answered the phone and expressed her sympathies, but Jean-Paul never called Simone. It was apparent that her brother was out of her life forever, just like her parents, and now, her husband.

Simone was only twenty-five, and had to start her life over again. But this time, as a widow. Joe's death was devastating. Everywhere she went, everything she saw in the apartment, reminded her of Joe.

"Mrs. Smith, I want to sell this apartment. What do you think? "

"I agree. It is time to remove yourself from these memories and start a new life. You can come to Charlottesville, and stay as long as you want. You know our home is your home. You can take care of the legal matters just as well in Virginia as you can in New York."

Simone called her boss and said she would not be returning; in fact, she was going to move out of state.

Mrs. Smith and Simone cleaned out her apartment, interviewed real estate agents, and packed up the few belongings and clothes she wanted to keep. Items Joe's family didn't want were donated to the Salvation Army. Her large, two-bedroom co-op in Tribeca was listed for $685,000. It sold in two days for $30,000 above the asking price. It was a cash offer, closing in 60 days.

After the contracts on the co-op were signed, Simone left the remaining legal matters in the hands of her New York attorney, Sidney Harding. He would keep her updated on the progress of the sale, as well as other matters regarding insurance claims, probate court, and the lawsuit against the taxicab company.

Simone was now ready to leave New York.

She and Virginia packed up Simone's Honda Civic Hatchback and drove to the Smith's home. Once again, Simone put her belongings in their garage and moved into their small guest room.

Henry said, "Take your time to figure out what it is you'd like to do. There's no rush. We're here for you."

Simone spent many days sitting on their porch, reading, healing, and journal writing. Many nights were spent crying herself to sleep. Six months after returning to Charlottesville, Simone took a trip back to Louisville to visit Mrs. Genet and Aunt Agnes. She hoped she would also see her brother and meet her two nieces. She was willing to give him one final chance. She called Jean-Paul twice, left a message on his answering machine. But he never returned her phone calls. She never called her brother again.

"Oh, Simone," Mrs. Genet said as she gently hugged her former neighbor. "It is so good to see you. Come in and tell me how you are doing. I'm so sorry to hear about Joe. What a pity, such a young man, so handsome."

At first, Simone found it difficult telling Mrs. Genet about the accident. Although it happened a year ago, it seemed fresh in her mind. She understood Mrs. Genet's need to know the facts. She wasn't being nosey. Rather, talking about it was helping Simone face the tragedy without collapsing into a sobbing heap. No, Mrs. Genet wasn't a "meddling old biddy" as Jean-Paul called her. She was a kind and caring woman, who loved both Simone and her mother.

From Mrs. Genet's house, Simone drove to her Aunt Louise, ten miles outside of town.

"I haven't seen or heard from your brother. It's sad he turned his back on his kinfolk. But that's what abusers do – they isolate themselves and their family from the outside world."

Simone wasn't surprised by her aunt's statement, but wanted to hear more. "What do you mean, Aunt Louise?"

"I'm sure Jean-Paul isn't much different from your father. I suspect he hits his wife, just like Phillipe did to my sister. Yes, I knew he was beating her. As the years went on, we saw less and less of her. I hadn't seen your parents for two years before the accident." Aunt Louise stopped talking and made the sign of the cross. "He didn't want us seeing her bruises, or us telling her to leave him. No, your mother was as stubborn as a mule. She must have felt she deserved the beatings. The more he drank, the more he beat her. The more he beat her, the less I saw her."

On her drive back to Charlottesville and the comforts of the Smith home, Simone realized she was facing a crossroad in her life. She could accept defeat, and stay with the Smith family, where she would be safe. Or, she could start a new life, in a different location. Unlike her mother, who didn't have the courage, and was masochistic, Simone felt courage stirring inside her. Simone recalled the **FEAR** poster from years ago, and her mantra her first few days at **NYU**: Face Everything And Rise.

It was time to move on.

CHAPTER 10

Therapy over the past year helped Simone work through the "firsts": the first Christmas, the first New Year's, and her first anniversary without Joe. She discussed the horrors of her childhood, and how memories impaled on her by the monster - her father - caused flashbacks. "Only time and therapy will help," the doctor said.

In August, while Judy was home from her job as a teacher in Richmond, Simone persuaded her to go with her to a wedding planner's convention in Washington, DC.

"It is time for me to go back to work," she told her friend. "I want to see how much the business has changed, and I want to make new contacts."

Judy and Simone were eager to be going on a road trip again. Although it wasn't as exotic or exciting as their trip to Paris years ago, Simone was looking forward to this time alone with her best friend.

Attending this convention were planners from all across the country. Those who organized high-end weddings to the stars, and those who planned weddings in church Bingo halls. One woman in particular, caught Simone's attention. Her name was Jennifer Keys, a wedding planner from Connecticut. She had a dry and off-beat sense of humor, which Simone liked. She wore very high heels, which Simone envied, and had the straightest blond hair, which Simone coveted over her own black curly hair. They connected almost immediately, and became inseparable during the rest of the convention.

There were remarkable historic similarities between Jennifer and Simone. Jennifer Keys was born and raised in Merrick, Long Island. Her mother Bridgette was a homemaker, who worked part time as a seamstress. Born in Dublin, she came to America with her parents in the

1940s. Not educated, but smart enough to know that her children needed to go to college, and strive to achieve the American dream. Bridgette tried to fit in with the other mothers in town, but was rejected often, being called "a lace-curtain Irish woman" behind her back.

Jennifer's father Patrick, also from Ireland, was a blue-collar worker at a tool manufacturing company. He worked long hours, and spent every Friday night at the local bar. Often, Jennifer and her brother Terrance were called to pick up their drunk father, and carry him home. He swore he'd never drink again, but the following Friday night he was back at the same bar, sitting on the same stool, drinking the same whiskey.

When Jennifer was eighteen, she left to go to college in Colorado. She came home occasionally to visit her parents, but was disgusted to see her father still drinking. Following in their father's footsteps, was her brother Terrance. Her heart went out to her mother, but there wasn't much she could do other than try to force her to leave and move away.

"I could never leave your father and brother. They need me so much. Who would cook and clean for them, and mend their clothing? No, my dear child. You go and have a wonderful life. I am happy here."

On the last night of the convention, Jennifer joined Simone and Judy for dinner in Georgetown. They ate raw oysters by the dozen, cracked open lobsters, staining their plastic bibs with lobster juice, and shared a bottle of prosecco. They swapped stories about demanding brides, and how they were all the same from New York to California. They laughed so hard that tears stung Simone's face. But this time, they were tears of laughter, and not pain.

"I'm working a large wedding at the New York Plaza Hotel on New Year's Eve," said Jennifer. "Wedding for about five hundred people . . . very high end . . . free room for two nights. I need an additional assistant. Interested? $4,500, plus travel expenses."

"Absolutely!" Simone answered without giving the offer much thought.

"I think it's a fabulous opportunity, Simone," Judy said. She smiled at her friend, hoping this would be just the beginning of her new life. She had suffered so much tragedy in such a short amount of time.

She had to be fingerprinted and have a background check done before Jennifer could hire her. "Client's requirement," noted Jennifer.

The wedding at the Plaza was a tremendous amount of work with a lot of moving parts, all of which Simone found exhilarating. The high stress level, working on a tight time schedule, and the use of her creative talents, brought back a renewed energy. Jennifer was impressed by Simone's ability to work with a demanding bride, her creativity, and ability to think quickly on her feet.

For the next six months the two women worked together. Simone continued living in Virginia and traveled up to New York, New Jersey or Connecticut to work with Jennifer. Afterwards, she'd return to Virginia where she would recharge. This routine worked well for Simone, and helped to bridge the gap from her grief into the next chapter of her life.

Then, in October of the following year, Jennifer called Simone and told her about an interesting opportunity.

"Hey, Simone. My boss is selling his event planning business. I do the weddings, but he does other events too - from corporate to kids' birthday parties. He has a good following of regular clients. There are two event planners on staff, but they're not able to buy the business. I thought you might be interested. I don't have the money - I spend it all on shoes." They both laughed.

Simone responded, "Is it possible for me to come up with my attorney to review his books? My attorney is in New York, so it shouldn't be a problem for him to get there."

"I'll find out for you. Jimmy, the owner, is retiring and moving to Florida; planning to leave by the end of the year. I'd say you could stay with me, but I only have a fold-out couch. There's a nice Hampton Inn nearby if you want to stay there."

Simone was quick to read between the lines. She didn't think Jennifer was interested in having her as a roommate for two or three nights. Besides, Simone liked her own space.

"I'd prefer to stay in a hotel. I don't want to scare you in the morning with my bedhead hair."

"And I don't want you to see me in slippers and know how short I really am."

Simone knew if she and Jennifer were going to work together in the future, there must be an invisible line of privacy between them.

CHAPTER 11

The meeting was held two weeks later in Jimmy's attorney's office in Westport, Connecticut. Simone's attorney, Sidney Harding, came up from New York City. Three hours later, Simone shook hands with Jimmy and told him she was interested.

"Of course, I have to do my due diligence before going forward," Simone said.

"Of course, Ms. Simpson," Jimmy answered.

The attorneys drew up papers. Explanations and required signatures followed. Simone and Sidney left with the promise of final contracts by the following week. They followed the meeting with lunch at Tarry Lodge, a block from the Westport train station. Simone devoured a generous serving of cavatelli with spicy sausage and tomatoes, and Sid enjoyed a substantial serving of eggplant parmigiana.

"I think it's a good asset Simone, and it's not a huge investment. Even if Jimmy has a second set of books, and he doesn't really have all those great clients, it's not a tremendous amount of money you'll be losing. You'll be able to build the business to your liking. It's good that the two staff people, Katy and Jonathan, are willing to stay on. Since they're both young, and eager to work and learn, I think they'll be an asset to your business. They represent consistency for the clients who don't like change, or the news about Jimmy's retirement. My advice would be that you keep them. Put them on a trial period for six months. See if you all like each other. If you do, keep them. I'd recommend you increase their menial salaries."

He continued, "This part of Connecticut is called the Gold Coast. There are a lot of wealthy, influential folks who live here. I think Jennifer would balance well as a business partner. She's the Yin to your Yang."

"Thank you, Sid. I was thinking the same thing. I'd like to figure out a way to make Jennifer a partner – maybe a 10% interest. Is that possible? The percentage would go up if the business flourishes. And yes, I'd like Katy and Jonathan to stay. I agree, their salaries are menial."

"Anything is possible, Simone. We just have to do the math. I need you to call Mary Ann, your financial advisor and tell her what you're planning to do. Between the two of us we'll make this a good, solid business decision for you. Meanwhile, I'll draw up a proposal and fax it over to your hotel. Read it over thoroughly, and fax it back to me at home. Talk to Jennifer and see what she thinks. We can modify the agreement to fit both your needs."

He added, "Have you thought about what you'd like to name the company?"

Simone paused for a moment before answering. "Yes, I have. I'd like to call it, "I Do" LLC.

"That's a fantastic name!" Sidney exclaimed. "I'll get on that paperwork as well."

They finished their meals, enjoyed a cup of cappuccino, and discussed Simone's decision to move up to Connecticut.

"I love Mr. & Mrs. Smith, but it is time, Sid. I think I need to leave the nest."

"I think you know Simone, it is extremely rare that a family like the Smith's comes along. They took you in when you needed them the most."

"Yes, I know. I must have done something right to be connected to them."

"By the way, I received a call from the attorney representing the taxicab company. They want to settle out of court for $25 million dollars. We filed suit against the taxicab company, and the driver, personally. Joe died as a direct cause of the driver, but you also lost his future income, and unfortunately, your unborn child. If you say no, it could take several more years before it comes to trial. Of course, you won't see all of that money, but a good sum of it. That, including your parent's estate from the sale of the house, Joe's double indemnity life insurance, your savings, and the co-op sale, you'll be quite set with over $15 million dollars in the bank. Even with all that, you will need to be careful. I've seen people blow through a fortune thinking it will always be there."

"Let me give the offer some thought. It is an exorbitant amount of money."

"It is at that. But don't take too long."

Simone gave Sid a big hug before he got on the train. "Sid, you've been an incredible rock and mentor to me.

"My pleasure, Simone. I only wish I had more clients like you."

Later that day, Sid faxed the document to purchase the wedding planning business to the Hampton Inn where Simone was staying. She spent the next two hours reading it and writing her questions in the margins before faxing it back to Sid. Then, she telephoned Jennifer and asked if they could meet at Centro's Ristorante for lunch later that week.

Jennifer ordered Chicken Milanese: Pecorino crusted juicy chicken breast, topped with a mound of peppery arugula, cherry tomatoes, croutons, shaved parmesan and herb vinaigrette. Simone ordered Salmon Nicoise: perfectly cooked salmon filet, served with string beans, tomatoes, boiled potatoes, briny olives, capers, a hard-boiled egg, and also dressed with herb vinaigrette. The meal reminded her of the night Joe proposed.

Over their enjoyable meals, they chatted.

"Jennifer, my attorney and I reviewed Jimmy's books. I've decided I would like to purchase the business. In addition, I would like you to be a partner with a 10% interest." Simone reached into her messenger bag and pulled out a sheaf of papers. "Sidney drew up the legal documents for your review. You don't have to answer right away; think about it. But I'd love to have you on board."

"Simone, I don't need time to think about it. Yes, I'd love to work with you, and be your business partner."

Legal documents were drawn up, signed, sealed and "I Do" LLC was created. After renovations to the office, including new desks, computers, carpeting, and a fresh coat of paint, Simone opened her business, with Jennifer as a 10% partner. They became the dynamic duo planners of weddings and events in Fairfield County, Connecticut.

Simone finally felt that after such a long hiatus, a new direction and a new life were in the forefront to occupy her thoughts. Her life with Joe was behind her. She had to think about creating a new chapter in her life, and moving forward.

The next step: Simone and Jennifer went house hunting. They began in Old Greenwich, Connecticut and looked at homes as far up the coast as Guilford. Simone felt the most comfortable in Westport. Growing up in Kentucky, she never had the opportunity to go to the beach. In Westport, she was steps away from the shore. It was a diverse community with a concentration of artists and writers. The home prices fit into her budget, and it was a short drive to the office.

She decided to purchase a rundown 1950s cottage on Compo Beach in Westport. She paid $550,000 cash for the house, spent another $200,000 on renovations, and another $125,000 working with an interior designer. The only people who knew about her finances were her attorney, her financial planner, and the Smith family. Not even Jennifer knew about her wealth, and Simone wanted to keep it that way.

CHAPTER 12

Simone and Jennifer drove out to the Bouvier home in Summit, New Jersey on a bright, but cold Sunday afternoon in April 2014. The initial meeting was to discuss dates, venue and food options, their "must haves" and to meet all the players involved. Most important in Simone's mind: to walk away with a signed contract.

Part of Simone's persona as a business woman was a professional-looking appearance, from the car she drove - a White Porsche Cayenne SUV - to her clothing, hair, jewelry and makeup . . . down to her purse and leather messenger bag.

The Bouvier's home, sitting on three acres of land, was an enormous 8,000 square foot French colonial style home with multiple columns and a balcony that wrapped around the second floor. While walking up the path to the front door, Jennifer did a quick count of fourteen oversized windows just in the front section of the home.

"I wonder who washes all those windows," whispered Jennifer.

They climbed the four white steps to the porch's landing. The two weather beaten rocking chairs swayed in the breeze. Nestled next to them were two wicker side tables, equally in need of some refurbishing. Simone imagined the rockers calling: "Come. Sit. Stay a while." She flashbacked to the Smith's home with their welcoming wrap-around porch. She felt a sudden pang of missing them.

Simone's daydream vanished when the front door swung opened. She and Jennifer were greeted by an elderly, gray-haired black gentleman wearing a dark blue suit. His bright, large, Chiclets-looking teeth didn't fit his wrinkled, small mouth, and were the main focus of his face. His brown eyes, slightly cloudy by milky cataracts, were welcoming.

"Miss Simone and Miss Jennifer?" he asked. "Right this way, please." They followed the butler at a snail's pace to the foyer where Mr. and Mrs. Bouvier were standing, waiting to greet the two women.

The wide pine floorboards were covered by a large, round Oriental rug. An antique drum table, featuring small drawers around the table's circumference was centered on the rug. Showcased on the table was a clear oval vase filled to capacity with freshly cut colorful spring flowers along with cat tails and pussy willows. Above the table hung an ornate brass and crystal chandelier that dated back to the early 1800s.

Mrs. Amanda Bouvier was a rotund woman about 5'3" with very short white hair and silver wire rimmed eyeglasses. She wore a multi-tiered powder blue dress that emphasized her width. Her neckline, graced with a triple strand pearl necklace, made her resemble Barbara Bush. Simone was sure that if she had the opportunity to rub those pearls against her teeth, she'd feel sand.

Mr. Bruce Bouvier, a man in his mid-60s was about six feet tall, slender, with salt and pepper hair. He looked very debonair, dressed in dark brown Dockers, a blue oxford styled shirt with rolled up sleeves that matched his eyes. His feet were covered with well-worn brown deck shoes. A bulldog-style pipe was nestled in the corner of his mouth. Smoke never rose from the bowl, but the pipe seemed to fit his persona well.

"Hello my dears," Mrs. Bouvier said in a syrupy voice as she rushed forward to shake their hands. "How very nice to meet you both. We've heard so much about you from our friends the Goldblatts. Bruce and I attended their son Arnie's wedding last year in Rye, New York, and it was just marvelous. I couldn't believe . . ."

"Mother," Bruce cut her off, "let the ladies catch their breath."

Nervously, she answered, "Oh, yes. Yes, of course. Come in ladies. Come in."

"Let's convene in the living room," instructed Mr. Bouvier. He took his wife's elbow and guided her and the wedding planners from the foyer to the living room. They sat down across from each other in uncomfortable antique white chairs, making small conversation about the weather, and the traffic going over the George Washington Bridge at all hours of the day and night. Simone and Jennifer made a point to gush over their lovely, tastefully-decorated home.

Whenever Mrs. Bouvier spoke, her eyeglasses slid down her ski-lift nose. Using her thumb and forefinger together, she raised the glasses back into place. From there, her hand glided down to her strands of pearls where she fondled them like worry beads.

Simone looked around the palatial-sized rooms. They were decorated in French Colonial style, featuring white, ornate pieces of furniture and large gold-gilded framed artwork. The home was immaculate, and reeked of very old money and an accompanying old-world lifestyle.

"Our daughter Casey-Ann recently got engaged to the Michaelson boy," announced Mrs. Bouvier. She said 'the Michaelson boy' as if Simone would know all the high society people of Summit, New Jersey. "They're thinking of having their wedding next year."

Simone interjected, "Let's wait until your daughter and her fiancé are here, then we can discuss their plans."

Casey suddenly bopped down the center staircase wearing faded jeans and a well-worn Princeton sweatshirt. Her blond hair was pulled back into a tight ponytail that swung in unison with the tail of a golden retriever at her feet. Simone was transported back to when she wore her hair exactly like that. Her father would reprimand her, "You need to see the blackboard. Don't look like a shaggy dog."

Everyone stood as she entered the room.

"Hi. I'm Casey." She shook hands with Simone and Jennifer with a limp, dead fish handshake. "Nice Louboutins."

"Thanks," Jennifer responded, not surprised that Casey would know and appreciate her taste in shoes.

While moving a stray blond hair out of Casey's face, Mrs. Bouvier announced, "Casey-Ann is our youngest and the last in the family to be married." Turning to her, she continued, "And it's about time, darling. In two more years you'll be thirty, and getting a bit too old to start a family," Mrs. Bouvier said, rubbing her pearls.

"Oh Mom, please," Casey mumbled in an annoyed tone, not looking back at her mother.

Simone and Jennifer gave each other a quick glance that spoke volumes. Simone thought Casey looked older than she apparently was.

Acting as a tour guide, Mr. Bouvier cleared his throat and suggested they head to the heated solarium. The glass enclosed room overlooked the soon-to-be opened pool and the deserted clay tennis court. Little heads of daffodils, tulips and other colorful spring flowers peeked through dirty, clumped snow, which couldn't melt fast enough for the blossoms in the large flower beds.

"Patrick should be here any moment," Mr. Bouvier informed Simone and Jennifer. "He's organizing a spring golf tournament at the club with his father."

As if on cue, they heard, "Hi everyone," as Patrick was led into the room by the butler. More introductions and handshakes followed. He gave Casey a quick peck on the cheek, her eyes blank with no emotion. She didn't seem to be an excited bride, thought Simone

Simone guessed him to be around thirty-five. He stood over six feet tall, and had a thin, slight build. He wasn't particularly handsome, not very muscular, just ordinary looking, with pockmarked skin. He had watery blue eyes and mousy brown hair.

"Do you have allergies, dear?" Mrs. Bouvier asked Patrick. "You've had the sniffles for an awfully long time."

"Yes. I do," he said in an unconvincing tone as he continued to sniffle. "You know, spring allergies."

Mr. Bouvier cleared his throat again, as any good tour guide would, as a signal for everyone to proceed to the next set of activities.

They adjourned to the solarium and sat down at a beautifully appointed table, covered with a peach-colored organza tablecloth, fine china, crystal glasses, and silver flatware. In the center was a crystal bowl of fragrant spring flowers matching the flowers in the entrance way.

Shortly after being seated, a painfully thin, slightly hunched over woman, possibly in her seventies, appeared from the kitchen. She had coarse white hair pulled back into a bun, no makeup, and she wore a maid's outfit. Simone guessed her to be from Jamaica, and much older than the elder Bouviers. Simone would bet she had been with the family for decades.

Following behind her was the butler. Both slowly brought out two dishes at a time. They presented a perfectly prepared dish of grilled chicken breast balanced on top of a generous salad of spring greens, dried cranberries, candied walnuts and thinly-sliced pears. The maid and butler never uttered a word or made eye contact with anyone.

When the last dish was placed in front of Patrick, Mrs. Bouvier said, "Thank you Gladys." The elderly woman, with apparent difficulty, slowly lifted her deeply wrinkled face. Her eyes showed no emotion. She smiled sublimely back at her employer. Her soft soled shoes glided her through the swinging door, and silently back into the kitchen, the same way she and the butler had entered the solarium.

After their luncheon they moved back to the living room. Simone said she and Jennifer would like to chat privately with Casey and Patrick to discuss their wedding. But Mrs. Bouvier didn't seem to get the hint. She settled herself down into an antique arm chair, too small for her width. She wedged herself into the chair like a woman refusing to accept she is now a size eight shoe instead of a seven. The fat around her hips moved up her body, past her waist, increasing her bust size by at least two inches.

"Whatever they want, I want. I just want my baby to be happy."

Mr. Bouvier got the hint and suggested, "Mother, come sit in the study and let the kids plan their wedding." She ignored his suggestion with the wave of her right hand as if to say, 'Don't bother me.' She was most likely afraid she couldn't get out of the chair without it being stuck to her as she walked. Mr. Bouvier went off to the study to read the rest of the New York Times, which was scattered on the floor and home to two sleeping golden retrievers.

"We were thinking of a June wedding," Casey announced. "Next year."

"Do you know how many guests?" Jennifer asked, her notebook poised with pen in hand.

Casey opened her mouth to speak, but it was Mrs. Bouvier's voice that answered, "Our guest list consists of four hundred fifty people. The same people we had at our son's wedding three years ago, and of course, Patrick's family." She said 'Patrick's family' with disdain in her voice and a slight wrinkle of her nose. More unspoken words between Simone and Jennifer.

"Our choices for a venue for that number of people are somewhat limited," Simone inserted before anyone else could interrupt. "We don't have much time, as most venues are booked a year and a half, sometimes two, in advance. Off the top of my head, there's the Borgata Hotel in Atlantic City, the Westmount Country Club in New Jersey, and the Grand Hamilton in Greenwich, Connecticut. All these venues are wonderful with high end amenities. There are other venues, of course, such as the Plaza in New York . . ."

Mr. Bouvier, still within earshot of what was being discussed, heard the words Atlantic City and dropped the newspapers on the floor. He bolted from his isolation in the study to join in the discussion. Holding his pipe in his right hand, he boomed as he walked into the living room, like an actor entering stage left.

"Oh no, not Atlantic City. We don't want people gambling our daughter's gifts away. Too sleazy an area. The Westmount, although very lovely, is where my brother had his son's wedding last year. I don't want them saying I copied their idea. Let's explore the Grand Hamilton. In Connecticut, you say Simone?"

A bit shocked by his commanding voice, Simone replied, "Yes, it overlooks Long Island Sound. It's in Greenwich, but there are other . . ."

Mr. Bouvier, looking more like a Shakespearian actor, continued his thinking out loud, "In Greenwich? That would work very well," he said as he began to pace back and forth, his brow furrowed.

He continued, "We have guests coming from New York City, New Jersey, Connecticut and Long Island. There are several flying in from California, Seattle, and two couples from London. And, of course, Patrick's family. Greenwich isn't too far from LaGuardia, Kennedy and the Westchester Airport. That would be most convenient."

He stopped his pacing, turned to his wife and asked, "Don't you agree, Mother?" But he didn't give Mrs. Bouvier a chance to answer.

He started up again, this time looking at Simone, "Can we perform the ceremony there as well? What about Father John from our parish, Mother. I wonder if he would oblige . . ." His words faded away as his thoughts took over. He placed his pipe back in his mouth as he continued to pace the room.

Casey and Patrick sat silently. The only sound between them was Patrick's continuous sniffling, and the occasional tapping on his cell phone.

Now Mr. Bouvier was taking over the wedding planning. He removed his pipe and said, "It wouldn't be fair to expect folks to drive to New Jersey for the ceremony, and then drive to Connecticut for the reception. Let's do it all in one place. Is that alright with you, sweetie?" he asked, as he focused on Casey.

Casey lifted her head to mumble, "That's fine. Whatever you and mom want. You're paying for the wedding."

"Casey and Patrick," Simone said with her voice directed at them. "I'd like to hear from you two. What would you like? After all, it's your wedding." Then, Simone crossed the proverbial line of: 'don't go there.' "I'd like both of you to concentrate on our discussion." Simone waited for the backlash. Silence. She thought she heard Mrs. Bouvier inhale an exasperated breath.

Casey glared at Simone as if to say, 'You're not my mother.'

Then she elbowed Patrick, who obviously didn't hear a word Simone said. He picked up his head, looked at Casey and she whispered, "She wants to talk to us."

Simone had the innate ability to recognize a loser when she saw one, and Patrick was a loser. He appeared to be going through the wedding motions as a disinterested participant. He couldn't care less where it was held, when it was held, or who was invited. Something about this couple didn't sit well with Simone. She wondered what their story was. She couldn't wait for the drive back to Connecticut so she and Jennifer could discuss their opinions privately.

Then Simone crossed the line again. "Mr. and Mrs. Bouvier, I'm going to ask that Casey and Patrick tell me how they envision their wedding day. You don't have to leave the room, but please hold your thoughts during this time. The ultimate goal is for each of them to marry the person with whom they want to spend the rest of their life. There are lots of details en route to that goal. I'd like to hear what they'd like on their wedding day, so reaching that goal can be a smooth transition."

In the subsequent silence, Simone heard the grandfather clock ticking, and the faint sound of dishes clattering in the kitchen.

Simone thought she killed the deal. But she had enough experience to know she was the one who had to satisfy their wants and needs. And if she didn't have their full cooperation, she would get blamed for everything that didn't go according to plan. She would rather know now with whom she was dealing, and vice versa.

Finally, the couple focused on what Simone was asking: what month, day, and time of day; type of dress; food; ceremony and vows; favors; flowers; invitations; music; photographers; videographers; registry; honeymoon; table settings; colors; place cards; theme; bridal party. . . the list was extensive. Simone was able to extract some very solid information from them, while Casey's parents sat like mute waxed figures, and Jennifer acted more like a court stenographer, taking copious notes.

"Now, Mr. and Mrs. Bouvier, I'd like to discuss my contract with you."

The Bouvier's were spellbound by Simone's take charge ability, and just nodded their heads in agreement.

"Casey and Patrick, if you'd like to stay during this segment, that's fine. But you don't have to." They fled from the room without a word and headed upstairs, with one of the dogs close behind. A few seconds later they heard a bedroom door slam shut.

While Simone discussed her contract and wedding insurance options with Mr. and Mrs. Bouvier, Jennifer called The Grand Hamilton Hotel and made an appointment for a tour that following Friday night.

"Well, the way it works with wedding insurance," Simone said, "each vendor has a limit as to the claim amount. Most have a maximum payment of $10,000. "I strongly recommend you consider taking out a policy. You never know if something goes wrong: the venue going out of business, a fire, or if the photographer or flowers don't show up. If you're interested after reading the literature, you can call the insurance agent directly."

"I think we should discuss this with our attorney, Mother."

Mrs. Bouvier nodded in agreement.

"Absolutely," agreed Simone.

Simone and Jennifer left the Bouvier's home with a signed contract and a $50,000 retainer check.

The following Friday, Mr. and Mrs. Bouvier signed a contract with the Grand Hamilton Hotel for $250,000.

CHAPTER 13

Simone believed in "paying it forward." In August of 2014, she called the General Manager, Charles Hamilton VI at the Grand Hamilton Hotel in Greenwich, Connecticut. "I'd like to discuss a wedding idea I have involving your hotel. Are you free this Wednesday at 2:00 to meet?"

"Sure Ms. Simpson. I'm available. I know you've worked several weddings here, and we appreciate you thinking of our facility. Can you tell me what this is about?"

"Can it wait until Wednesday? I have to get to another meeting. I'll see you then." Simone had become the quintessential assertive businesswoman.

Two days later, she arrived at the hotel for her meeting where Mr. Hamilton was waiting for her in the lobby.

He was wearing a gray uniform, with a stark white shirt and black tie, his brass-colored nametag, **CHARLES**, was anchored on his right breast pocket.

Simone approached him. In one quick glance, he drank in her appearance, and she, his. Fashionably dressed, she wore a pale blue linen skirt that ended just above her knees, a beige sleeveless blouse, and a double strand of long pearls that bounced against her breasts. Her shoulder was adorned by a Dooney & Bourke bag, and her heels clicked on the marble as she walked towards him.

They shook hands and exchanged pleasantries. He directed her to a small conference room off the lobby, and motioned for her to take a chair by the window overlooking Long Island Sound.

"Would you like some coffee, or tea?"

"No. No, thank you," she answered.

"I hope you don't mind if I make myself a cup. It's been a long day, and I'm on duty until well past eight o'clock." Silence in the room was broken by the gurgling machine, and the final swoosh of steam.

"How can I help you, Miss Simpson? And please, call me Charlie." He blew on his coffee and cautiously took a sip.

"Okay, Charlie. And you can call me Simone. For the past two years I've been volunteering at a cancer center in lower Connecticut. One of the patients is a brave twenty-four year old woman with terminal cancer. I sat and talked to her while she was receiving her treatment, and we've become friends. When I told her I'm a wedding planner, she said it is her dream to have a wedding. But she and her fiancé don't have the money. Her funds go towards medical bills."

Simone continued, "She'd like to have a simple, traditional wedding. She wants to wear a wedding gown, have her dad walk her down the aisle, and be able to dance her first dance with her husband. The reason I'm here, Charlie, is because I'd like to provide a wedding for her free of charge. And hopefully, the Grand Hamilton Hotel will support me with this endeavor."

While Simone was talking, Charlie was becoming more and more intrigued with her exotic looks, mesmerized by her green eyes, and hint of a slight southern accent.

Although they had worked together on several weddings, their direct contact had been very limited. This was the first time they were in personal contact, and alone in a room with the door closed. He found himself enjoying every minute.

It took him a few seconds to realize Simone had stopped talking. To cover his embarrassment, he finished his coffee, and picked up a pen and started clicking the top. "Well, that sounds very charitable, Miss Simpson . . . I mean, Simone. How can the Grand Hamilton Hotel help you?"

Before she continued, she stared at the pen. He put it down on the desk, and placed his hands on his lap.

"I was thinking if she had a reception on an off day, such as a Wednesday, would the hotel donate the venue? I'm willing to pay for the food, drinks, invitations, flowers, the musicians, her wedding dress, cake, photographer and honeymoon . . . basically, everything, other than the venue rental and staff."

"I'll have to check with upper management, of course," Charlie responded. He left out that 'upper management' meant his father. "But I'm sure we can arrange a lovely wedding. I'd be happy to work with you, and do everything I can to limit your financial exposure. You've got a great sense of giving back, Simone. And an impressive entrepreneurial mind as well. Your idea is extremely generous."

Simone felt her cheeks growing warm, embarrassed by his compliments.

The silence was palpable. Neither one of them spoke as they checked each other out in a discreet, yet obvious way.

She smiled at him, taking an even closer look at him. He was rather handsome and well-built. He had kind brown eyes, thick brown hair with a hint of grey at the temples. No wedding band. Simone felt a stirring inside her that caused another flash of heat to shoot through her body. At this point, her cheeks were becoming flushed while small beads of sweat formed on her upper lip.

Noticing the shift in her appearance, Charlie asked, "Are you ok, Simone? Would you like some water?"

"Yes, please. It's rather warm in here," she said. "August heat." The angrier she got at herself for revealing her feelings to Charlie, the hotter her face felt.

Charlie left the conference room. As soon as the door closed behind him, Simone grabbed a piece of paper from the desk and started fanning herself. She took out a tissue and dabbed at her upper lip.

Charlie arrived with a bottle of cold San Pellegrino. "I hope this helps."

"Yes, thank you," Simone opened the bottle and took a long swig, ignoring the paper cup that was placed next to the San Pellegrino.

"I've been running on empty these past few weeks, and I think things are starting to catch up with me," she explained. She took another long swallow. "Let's go back to discussing this wedding. When do you see an opening in the hotel's schedule? Since the bride has limited time – literally - I'd prefer to have this wedding take place within the next few months."

Charlie walked over to the desk, wiggled the mouse to wake up the computer, and checked the hotel's schedule. Simone stood behind him. The scent of White Diamonds wafted over them, and Charlie inhaled the intoxicating aroma. He refocused on the screen. "We are booked solid until Thanksgiving. If she's interested, we can do a traditional Thanksgiving dinner with turkey, stuffing, and the fixings, plus other traditional foods. It certainly would be a very special holiday for her and her family." He swung around in his chair and looked up at Simone. "This might sound morbid, Simone, but I think they'd rather see her alive than when she's in a coffin."

"I agree. Good point, Charlie. What about the chefs and the staff? Will they be willing to work that day?"

He rose from the chair and stood a mere foot away from Simone. He looked directly into her green eyes, mesmerized. "They get paid time and half on holidays, so some will fight for the time. Besides, if the wedding is early enough, the staff can still have dinner with their families."

He hesitated a moment, then fishing about her personal life said, "I hope this won't hamper your family's Thanksgiving plans. I'm sure you'll be busy with your husband that day."

"No, I won't be busy." She stared back, equally mesmerized by his brown eyes. "I'm not married, and my parents have passed on. What about you – won't your wife be angry that you're working on Thanksgiving?"

The mutual flirtations were in full bloom, and Simone could feel her face redden again.

"I'm ok working that day," Charlie responded. "In fact, it will be nice to do a wedding like this. We always have one or two managers on site for a holiday, in case of a last minute booking."

"What about Plan B, Charlie? What if the bride dies right before the wedding?"

"No worries. If she dies a few days before, we'll freeze what we can, cook the turkeys and donate them to a soup kitchen. She'll live to see her beautiful wedding day. And with you orchestrating it, there's no chance of anything going wrong."

"Great. I'll check with my bride and see what she thinks about having her wedding on Thanksgiving." Simone extended her hand, hoping it wasn't perspiring.

His response was equally warm and welcoming. They shook hands slowly while staring into each other's eyes. No words were spoken.

His voice lowered, almost to a sexy whisper, "It certainly has been a great pleasure seeing you again, Simone. I look forward to working closely with you. I'll email you once I hear what the hotel can do to contribute to the wedding. I'm sure you'll be very pleased."

What was it about this man that stirred such feelings, Simone wondered? It had been so long since these kinds of emotions had surfaced. She felt titillated, yet frightened.

CHAPTER 14

After the meeting at the Grand Hamilton Hotel, she went directly to the hospital to discuss plans with the bride and her parents. The three cried.

"If I live long enough, I'd love to have my wedding on Thanksgiving. The Grand Hamilton Hotel? Are you sure Simone? Are you really sure? That would be a dream come true. You're an angel sent from Heaven. Thank you."

"It is my pleasure, Carol. We'll talk to your doctors to see if there are any limitations. And if you're well enough, I'd like to be able to send you and your husband on a honeymoon, even if it's only for three days, and close by. The Berkshires, perhaps. You've been through a lot and you deserve a break."

The following week Simone met with Carol and her doctors. She explained the wedding plans, but was concerned if Carol had limitations.

"As long as you can take all the stress of planning a wedding off Carol's back, she should be fine. Let the excitement and joy of a wedding be the only thought now. She's been an incredible patient who is responding very well to treatment." Carol's doctor turned to Simone. He gave her a sturdy, warm handshake. "I wish more people were as giving as you, Simone. You've made Carol so happy."

He turned to Carol. "Now Missy, you need to let Simone, your mother and Jason work on the wedding. No worries for you. I'm sure they'll create a beautiful day for you."

"Yes, doctor, I understand," Carol said like a child being reprimanded. Then she burst forth, "Can you come to the wedding, doctor? Can you?"

"You see, you're getting too excited already," he said with a grin.

Carol left the meeting with renewed energy and optimism.

I just hope she makes it to the wedding day, Simone thought.

Simone called her vendors, most of whom were not available to work that day, but figured out alternative approaches. Her favorite musician was busy, but he said he would send a 'B-List' DJ. "You'll love him. He's young, and he'll get the folks up and dancing." The photographer said he'd send an intern who will do a great job – guaranteed. "He's been studying with me for six months, he's a great photographer," he assured Simone. The florist said she could not help Simone, but suggested that she purchase the flowers online. As it turned out, purchasing them online was a wonderful recommendation. They were fresh, abundant, and delivered directly to the hotel the day before the wedding.

The bride's uncle was the pastor at Carol's church, and said he'd be honored to perform the ceremony. He had a booming and commanding voice, announcing, "It'll be a great opportunity to spend Thanksgiving with my family. Most of them stay clear away from me. I think they fear I'll convert them while they have turkey stuffed in their mouths," he said to Simone with a chuckle.

Simone called a dress designer she knew, who said she'd be happy to donate a "sample" wedding dress for the bride. Since sample size gowns were often a size two or four, the dress fit Carol's thin body as if it were made just for her. Minor alterations were required, which the seamstress did for free.

Charlie emailed Simone saying the hotel would donate the venue and cover the cost of the staff. Simone was delighted, both with the hotel's generosity, and with Charlie keeping his word that she would be pleased.

And pleased she was. She was also cautious for the feelings stirring inside her towards Charlie.

The wedding was held on Thursday, November 27, 2014, at the Grand Hamilton Hotel. One-hundred and fifty people witnessed Carol and Jason exchange their vows. When spoken, "...for better or for worse, in sickness and in health..." there were audible cries in the room, including tears shed by the couple. Even her uncle stopped the ceremony for a moment to wipe away a tear.

Simone and Charlie stood in the back of the banquet hall while the couple exchanged their vows. Simone was thinking about Joe, whom she still loved and missed every day. He had been taken from her nine years ago, but the pain could resurface easily. No one could ever touch her heart as he did. Simone also thought about Carol's husband, Jason. She knew the pain he would face when Carol died. But he would have time to prepare, and to say goodbye.

Charlie thought about his wife, and how miserable they both were in their marriage. They had nothing in common any longer. She was more in love with the Hamilton name and the Hamilton money, than with him. He knew their marriage was over. It was just a matter of time. Soon, he thought.

The end of a marriage is different from the death of a spouse. While they both deal with loss when a spouse dies, there is no one on the other end of the phone to say "good night."

Carol and Jason then left on a three-day honeymoon to the Gateways Inn in Lenox, Massachusetts. Charlie had comped the bridal suite for their first night together.

Yes, Simone thought, not only did Charlie have kind eyes, but also a kind heart.

It was 4:30 pm and Simone decided to go to the bar and decompress.

Charlie saw her, and asked, "Simone, do you have dinner plans?"

"No, I don't. I thought I'd have a drink, and then head to my hotel."

"Your hotel?"

"Yes, I'm staying at the Hampton Inn down the road. I'm driving to Virginia tomorrow, so staying in Greenwich cuts time off the trip."

"Why didn't you tell me you needed a room? I would have put you up here."

"Oh no, Charlie. Although I love this hotel, it doesn't match my pocketbook. I just spent a mini-fortune on today's wedding. I like to splurge, but not that much."

"Simone, call the Hampton Inn. It's before 6:00. Tell them you're going to cancel your reservation. Stay here. I'll comp you a room."

"I can't Charlie. Thanks, anyway."

"Can you have dinner with me?"

"I'd like that. I haven't had anything to eat since this morning."

"Great," Charlie responded, his face and eyes lighting up.

They were seated by the windows in the Tavern Restaurant over-looking the hills covered with a dusting of snow. They both ordered poached salmon beurre blanc with roasted autumn vegetables, and de-lighted in a bottle of Prosecco. Dessert was warm molten lava cake with a scoop of vanilla bean ice cream, accompanied by a Single Malt Scotch for Charlie, and Limoncello for Simone.

Simone tried to keep the conversation light, but she was curious. "Charlie, don't you have family you're supposed to be with tonight?"

"Yes, and no. My father, who owns the hotel goes to Florida for Thanksgiving. His wife – my step mother – has kids in Naples. My wife goes to her parents' for Thanksgiving. I can't stand them, and they can't stand me. It's a win-win."

"So, you are married," she blurted out. After a moment, she added, "I'm sorry, Charlie, I didn't intend to be nosy."

"It's not a good marriage. I spend most of my time here at the hotel just so I don't have to be at home. We tried working on our problems, but it's complicated."

After a brief silence, he continued, "Simone, I'm sure lots of men say, 'my wife doesn't understand me.' My wife Eve understands my money more than me. May I ask, you said you're not married, but is there a man in your life? You're a very attractive, successful woman. I'm sure you can have any man you want."

Simone paused for a moment, surprised at how at ease she felt talking to Charlie about her personal life . . . a man she hardly knew. "It's not the first time I've been asked that question. My husband was killed in an accident nine years ago. I haven't found anyone who can come close to him."

As they sipped their after-dinner drinks, nonverbal looks between them spoke volumes.

"Well, I think I should be getting to my hotel. I have a long drive ahead of me tomorrow. Thank you for all your help with Carol's wed-ding. And for dinner."

They parted ways, Simone off to the Hampton Inn, and Charlie to the bar for another Scotch.

After Simone left the hotel, Charlie noticed her black messenger bag was left near the leg of the table. A wishful thought crossed his mind: did she leave it on purpose, so he'd find it and would return it to her hotel room? He picked it up, grabbed his coat, and drove to the Hampton Inn. He kept his overcoat buttoned so that the receptionist wouldn't notice his Hamilton Hotel uniform.

"Ms. Simpson's room, please," he said.

"Is Ms. Simpson expecting you?"

"Yes, she asked me to bring her some documents," he said, as he held up the messenger bag.

The receptionist called her room to confirm.

Charlie found his way, and gently knocked on the door.

She opened the door, wearing only her bathrobe, and said seductively, "I was hoping you'd get the 'message.' Come in."

The door closed behind him. They stared at each other for a moment. Silent approval. He walked towards her and kissed her passionately. Reaching behind, she shut off the lights.

Simone let her robe drop to the floor. Her hunger, kept bottled up for so many years, could not be quelled. Their lovemaking went on for hours, broken by short naps, only to continue again. Finally, they collapsed in each other's arms and fell into a deep sleep.

At 5:30, Simone awoke, showered, and got dressed.

By 6:45, she was driving over the George Washington Bridge, heading to Virginia. Charlie was headed for another round of blissful dreams.

Chapter 15

Eve Marie Haggerty was born in the 'back country' of Greenwich, Connecticut. She and her parents lived in a small four-room cottage on the 75 acre estate of the Everly Family, prominent owners of a jewelry and gem company in New York's Diamond District. Eve's father was the groundskeeper, taking care of the specimen gardens and the greenhouse filled with orchids and other exotic plants. In addition, he supervised the other caretakers who oversaw the pools, tennis court and stables. Eve's mother was the cook, housekeeper, mender of clothing, and wiper of runny noses of the seven Everly children, all boys.

Eve was forbidden from playing or socializing with the Everly children. Often left to find her own amusement, the Everly children would tease her and call her a 'half-Everly,' as the first three letters of her name matched theirs. But their social status was monetary letters apart.

When asked if she was an only child, Eve nodded yes. What she wanted to say was, "Yes, I'm a lonely-only child." She was taught to obey orders given by the Everly family, and to always say, "Yes or No, Ma'am or Sir." She would often cry to her mother that the Everly boys were mean to her, calling her names, or pulling her hair. Her mother reminded her to stay clear of the family, and to be grateful she was able to grow up on this estate.

Once, while the Everly family was in Europe on summer vacation, Eve, age twelve, snuck into the stables. She lied to the stable hand saying the Everly family told her she could ride anytime she wanted. He saddled up one of the horses, lifted her up, and gave the animal a firm smack on its rump. The stallion took off with Eve on top, a grand smile across her face, the wind blowing through her long blond hair. She felt free. She felt like an Everly.

The three minutes of exhilarating freedom came to an abrupt halt when a large milksnake crossed their path, frightening the horse. He reared up and threw Eve to the ground. The horse galloped back to the stable, the snake slithered into the bushes, and Eve was left on the ground, crying out in pain. The handler remounted the horse, rode to Eve and brought her back to the house. She suffered a sprained wrist, and a broken rib. But the most pain came from her father's belt-beating across her legs and backside.

Her parents were compensated well for their hard work, but they never owned property, or were able to send Eve to one of the private schools in the area. She envied the lifestyle of the Everly family, dreaming, and scheming to one day live like them.

By the time Eve was seventeen, she learned how to use her body and good looks to get what she wanted, including access to the 'forbidden' areas of the Everly home and to Chad Everly's bedroom. When his parents were out and his siblings were occupied, he would sneak Eve up to his bedroom. Being the eldest of the children, he had his own small apartment located on the far end of the estate. There, he taught Eve the wonders of sex and she satisfied his kinky desires.

One of her demands in exchange for satisfying Chad's desires, was to get her name on the guest list to one of the social dances at the country club. He agreed to bring her, not as his date, but as a friend visiting from out of state. It was an unwritten rule amongst the rich of the back country of Greenwich to 'never date below your monetary status.' If they arrived separately no one would know that she was with him. He did not want his parents to find out she came holding his arm.

It was at this dance, Eve met Charles Hamilton VI, the grandson of the owners of the Grand Hamilton Hotel.

Eve was dressed in a strapless blue dress that enhanced her figure and matched her large blue eyes. Her hair, worn in a chignon, accented her long, flawless neck. It didn't take much for Charlie to become enchanted by her beauty. She had never been to one of the social events before, so her appearance was new and exciting to the men in the room. Whispers of, "Who is that beauty?" were heard.

She met Charlie's eyes, purposely picking him out of the crowd. She had read about his family's wealth in the local paper, and saw photographs of him holding the coveted polo cup. She knew what he could do for her. And she was willing to do things for him . . . anything he wanted . . . to get what she wanted.

She approached him, commanded his attention, and suggested they take a walk in the garden. They walked along the path to the far off area of the grounds, passing couples who sneaked off for a make-out session. They stopped near the rustic boundary fence between the country club's property and another estate. Charlie asked her where she lived . . . why hadn't he seen her before at these socials . . . and most importantly, was she attached to anyone?

She told Charlie she and her family lived on the Everly estate, stretching the truth by saying her parents were the house managers; not the groundskeeper and housekeeper.

"You're asking too many questions, Charlie. I'd prefer your lips were doing something else." She began kissing him, and before he realized, she had lowered the upper portion of her dress. She was only eighteen, but was experienced – lessons taught by Chad Everly.

Before the evening was over, Eve Marie Haggerty owned Charlie Hamilton's mind and body. Now, she had to work on owning his money.

For weeks after that event, Eve and Charlie secretly dated. She was certain Charlie's father would do everything possible to end their relationship. She convinced Charlie to get her a job at the Grand Hamilton Hotel. "I'll be a waitress, just as long as I'm near you." Charlie worked as a caddy and didn't have much influence, but he convinced the banquet manager to hire her, saying she was a good worker, and pleasant to look at.

After six months of working in the banquet hall, Eve finagled her way from temp to secretary in the corporate office. There, she snooped, observed and eavesdropped on matters concerning the family's wealth. She continued to entertain Charlie with her sexual exploits in the woods, and Chad in his bedroom.

That fall, Eve told Charlie she was pregnant with his child. (Or, was it Chad's? She didn't know.) Calculating who would provide her with the most opulent lifestyle, she decided it was Charlie's child. Her parents still worked for the Everly family, and if she declared the child to be Chad's, her parents would lose their jobs and possibly become homeless. No, Charlie was the logical choice to satisfy the standard of living she craved. One day Charlie would take over the Hamilton estate, shared with his two sisters. But Chad would have to share his parents' estate with six brothers. The Hamilton estate was three hundred acres, the Everly estate was only seventy-five.

Chad was furious with Eve when she told him she was marrying Charlie Hamilton. "I'll tell my parents about our secret rendezvous. Better yet, I'll tell Charlie."

But Eve was steps ahead of him. "Go ahead, Chad. Tell them . . . tell Charlie, and I'll say you raped me. I'm pregnant with Charlie's baby. But I can easily say it is your child. I'll destroy your life."

"I'll get your parents fired."

"Fine. They'll come live in the Hamilton mansion with Charlie and me. Everyone will know you threw them out because you're the father of my child. My mother won't have to play nursemaid to your entitled siblings. And my father can take care of the Hamilton grounds, and no longer kowtow to your father's demands." Fortunately, Chad believed her lies, and acquiesced.

Charlie and Eve's wedding was held at the Grand Hamilton Hotel, attended by elite socialites, dignitaries and members of their country club – the same club where the Everly family were members. Eve made sure only the Everly parents were invited, and not their children.

No one other than Charlie and Chad knew that Eve was pregnant. On their honeymoon in Los Cabos, Eve got her period. She told Charlie she had a miscarriage. At twenty years old, he didn't know what needed to be done if a woman had a miscarriage. He was disappointed, but too immature to fully understand the impact. "We're young, we have lots of time to have children," he said.

Charlie didn't know Eve was never pregnant, or that she had told him that simply to get herself into the Hamilton family. She had no intentions of ruining her beautiful figure by carrying a child, or staying home raising them. She married the Hamilton money, and she intended to enjoy it as much as possible.

As the years continued, Eve protected herself from getting pregnant just as she did before she got married.

After nine years of marriage, Charlie's father asked, "You know, Charles, it is the tradition for the Hamilton estate to be passed on to an heir. You have a long life ahead of you, you're only twenty-nine but I would think by now you and Eve would have produced a child, a Charles Hamilton VII."

"Don't you think this is a conversation I should be having with my wife and not my father?"

"Charles, I see I still need to teach you the ways of our family, of inheritance, and of life."

But Charlie cut his father off, and said, "This conversation is over. I have to get back to work." Charlie knew his wife didn't seem interested in having children. Every time the subject came up, she swore she was trying and quickly change the subject.

Once, when Charlie was looking for his misplaced watch, he rummaged through Eve's dresser. His heart dropped when he found a round container of birth control pills. Anger rose as he wondered if she claimed to be pregnant as a way to force him to marry her.

He sat in his large leather chair in the master bedroom, and wept. He was such a fool. So many questions were answered: why she got pregnant once, and never again, why she never encouraged them to see a fertility doctor, and her nonchalant attitude towards starting a family.

That evening, over dinner in the Tavern, Charlie said as she drank her second glass of wine, "Eve, do you think it's wise to be drinking alcohol while trying to get pregnant? In fact, you might already be pregnant."

"Doctors now believe that a glass or two of wine while pregnant is good for the baby."

Charlie hesitated for a moment, but forged ahead. "I found your birth control pills today," he said in a monotone voice. "You've been deceiving me all these years, haven't you?"

She was silent. She finished her glass of wine, and stared at Charlie. She lifted her hand and snapped her fingers for the waiter. "Another glass of Chardonnay, please," she said with an overly friendly smile.

She turned back to Charlie. "What were you doing snooping in my dresser?"

"I was looking for my watch. I happened to come upon the pill case. Eve, were you pregnant when we first got married?"

"Oh, but of course, my love," she said with a snarky tone. "You don't think I would have married you under false pretenses, do you? That would be grounds for an annulment."

His anger stewed, bubbling inside him like acid. She was more clever than he had thought. He sat back, and in an instant, his love for her turned to hatred.

He was now the General Manager at the Grand Hamilton Hotel. Over the years he worked his way up through the ranks, just like every other Hamilton. As his position rose, so did his earnings, which Eve spent.

"Hi Eve." The voice came from Michael, one of the tennis pros on the grounds. Eve's face lit up with excitement.

"Hi Michael. Nice to see you. You know Charlie, don't you?" Charlie noted she did not introduce him as her husband. The two men nodded in recognition. "I'll see you tomorrow morning," she said brightly.

Charlie kept his temper under control. How could he have been so stupid? He was lured in by her great body and her charm. The last decade of his life was a fraud; years he would never get back. Charlie realized his days of being married to Eve were numbered.

"Eve, I think we should consider going to a marriage counselor."

"I'm not interested," she answered quickly, without much thought. "I like being married to you," she added.

"You like being married to the Hamilton name," he snapped.

She smiled back at him.

It took a lot of control to keep his voice low, "That's it. You never loved me, but loved the idea of being married to the Hamilton money. You enjoy the amenities of the hotel, having the Hamilton name, and the luxury of openly flirting with others."

"Jealous?"

Charlie kept his mouth shut. His anger continued to rise, but he wouldn't give her the benefit of seeing his emotions.

"I want you to move out, Charlie. I want a separation." Eve announced while indulging in her fourth glass of wine. "You can live in the hotel. I'm not interested in sharing your bed any longer."

"Why don't you move out?" he asked, finding it difficult to keep his anger under control.

"No, I don't think so, Charlie. Why don't you explain your tryst to your father? I'm sure he'll understand why I've thrown you out. I know about that wedding planner. I know all about her."

"You don't know anything, Eve."

"I heard you and she were having dinner after working a charity wedding. You seemed quite entranced by her."

Who the hell could have told her this wondered Charlie. "What's so unusual about having dinner with someone after working an event?"

"On Thanksgiving? Please, Charlie. I'm not stupid. You said you were coming to my parent's place after you worked the wedding. You left the hotel, but you never showed up at my parent's home. We waited dinner for you. I was so embarrassed."

"Spare me the drama, Eve. Your parents can't stand me. It was probably the best Thanksgiving you had with your parents in years. Your mother wanted you to marry one of the Everly boys, not someone who runs a 'bed and breakfast' as your father calls the hotel. Yes, I had dinner with the wedding planner. She is a caring woman who gave up her holiday to provide a wedding for a dying woman. She's generous, unlike you, who just takes and takes, and never gives. Who told you I had dinner with her?"

"I have my spies."

"I'm sure you do. Well, there's nothing going on with her, or anyone else," he lied. He hadn't stopped thinking about Simone since that night of unbridled passion. "I'm a married man," he snapped without conviction.

Silence ensued for a few moments.

"Eve, I think, for once, you might be right. I'll move out. I'll talk to my father about giving me a room at the hotel. Maybe living apart for a while will give us time to think."

"You gave up rather quickly, Charlie. Did I hit a nerve?"

Charlie looked at her. "You disgust me." He threw down his napkin onto the table. He left the restaurant, went back to his home and packed. He couldn't wait to get away from Eve, a manipulative, cunning woman who played him for a fool.

Charlie called the hotel and booked the suite on the Executive Level – his new living quarters. Yes, he had acquiesced, but fighting with Eve was useless. This also gave him the freedom to pursue Simone. He knew she was the planner for the Bouvier wedding taking place in a few weeks. He couldn't wait to see her, to be with her, maybe repeat the night they spent together months ago. . .

"Mr. Hamilton, your father is on the phone," said Mrs. Gregory, the housekeeper, snapping Charlie out of his fantasies.

CHAPTER 16

"Can you believe it? In a few days we'll be married," Patrick said. You'll be my wife and we won't have to sneak around any longer. And you can quit your stupid job in the psych ward."

"Quit my job?" Casey snapped as she sat up and started putting on her shirt.

"Oh come on, honey. Don't get dressed. No one can see us out here in the woods. Besides if they do, we're getting married soon."

"What a time to tell me that you want me to quit my job," Casey said.

"I thought that was understood from the beginning. Between my folks and yours, we will have enough money so you can stay home and have kids."

"Kids. Who said anything about having kids? I've worked hard to get my Master's degree. I don't want to give all that up." What Casey was really thinking was, she'd lose access to her pills.

"Let's discuss this on our honeymoon." Patrick knew he had crossed boundaries. All he needed was for Casey to change her mind about getting married. He spent three long years wooing this bitch for her family's money and he was not going to jeopardize that now.

"Hey, I know what you'd like," Patrick said, trying to change the subject. If there's one thing in this world that Casey Ann Bouvier could never say no to was a snort of coke.

Patrick took out his little zippered case and presented Casey with what she wanted, more than him. He could see it in her eyes. *I wish her eyes would light up like that when she looked at me,* he thought.

Casey took a long snort of the line of fine powder, looked at Patrick and said, "That was very nice."

Patrick and Casey met at college. She was the head cheerleader, and he was the king of the frat house; the party guy, the "supplier." He barely made it through college, graduating with a C average. Some of his professors couldn't figure out how he was still able to stay in school, but assumed his daddy's money spoke louder than grades.

His first summer after graduation, Patrick went to a rehab center in Colorado for six weeks. His parents kept it very hush-hush saying their son wanted to travel for a while after college. When he went for his second stay at a rehab center, they said he was doing a semester abroad.

His parents' money went to two places: up their son's nose, and to rehab centers. After his second stay at a rehab in Arizona, his father told Patrick that he was being cut off.

"We've had enough of you burning our money. Your trust fund has been suspended, and your inheritance will be held in escrow unless you're clean for at least seven years. Meanwhile, you will be required to take impromptu drug tests. You'll have to get a job and make your own way in life."

Patrick couldn't believe what he was hearing. His father and mother were cutting him off? What sort of hell was he living in?

He had to figure out his future. He needed access to money. He needed his daily fix. The one name that came to mind was Casey. He wondered if she was still available. After they had graduated college, they had gone their separate ways. She to continue her education, and he to continue his love of drugs. Two years after graduation and two rehab stints later, he reconnected with Casey playing the role of the interested suitor. But he was really interested in dating her family's money. She had recently broken up with someone she had dated in college, a has-been jock. She was available and interested in reigniting the spark between them. And Patrick's family status is what Casey loved.

With his father's influence and help, Patrick got a job as a back office clerk at a Wall Street investment banking firm. It was probably the biggest mistake Mr. Michaelson ever made, but he felt this was the last chance he could give his son to make it on his own.

Patrick had it all – a solid job on Wall Street and Casey as his arm candy. But it wasn't too long before he fell back to his old ways. He hung out and partied with the real money makers, the traders.

The drinking led to a toke here and there, and before he knew it, Patrick was back to snorting crack. Casey worked at a center for mentally challenged patients, and was drug-tested frequently, so she was careful not to indulge too often. Cocaine stayed in the urine for two to four days, so she was careful about when she snorted. When she applied for her job at the state mental health institute, she informed her employer that she was in a severe car accident, and was still on pain-killers; probably would be for the rest of her life.

In the fall of 2012, Casey had been driving intoxicated and on drugs, when she drove through a Stop sign and slammed her SUV into another car. The sedan that Casey had hit was being driven by a young woman with a one-year-old baby in a car seat in the back passenger side.

The police said, "You're very lucky, Mrs. Bartók. If the baby was in the car seat directly behind you, we might have had a different outcome. Meanwhile, you'll need to spend several weeks in the hospital recovering from your injuries. Do you have someone who can take care of your baby while you're in hospital?"

"Yes, officer. My mother can help me. She'll be here soon."

In order to avoid a lengthy trial, Mr. Bouvier had paid Mrs. Bartók $250,000 cash to make the whole situation disappear and to avoid a trial.

One night while waiting for Casey to arrive at their regular spot on Chambers Street, the bartender asked Patrick, "What's your desire?" Patrick hesitated a moment and looked at the bartender. He was new. He glanced at his name tag. GREG. Patrick stared at his mesmerizing large black eyes, rich ebony skin, and large moist lips. What was he asking me . . . do I want a drink, drugs or something else he wondered?

"I'm not sure," he responded. His mind was racing, trying to figure out his weird attraction to this guy. Maybe because he looks exotic, or maybe it's the snort I did a little while ago that's playing with my mind?

"What would you like?" Greg repeated.

"What are you offering?" Patrick said in a whisper.

"Whatever your heart desires."

Patrick was titillated. In a low voice, so no one around could hear him, he asked, "Got any blow?"

"Depends on what sort of blow you want," came the quick response.

Patrick was suddenly aroused. What the hell was going on? He never felt this way towards a guy. Sure, there was joshing in the locker room back in college, but that was just the guys fooling around. This was different. This was provocatively exciting.

"Meet me tomorrow night. I get out of here at midnight." Greg slipped Patrick his address on a napkin.

"Midnight? That's late. I live in Jersey . . ."

"If you're interested, you'll be there." Then Greg placed a Bud Lite in front of him and walked away to help another customer.

"Hey, how did you know I drink Bud Lite?"

"I'm observant," Greg answered without turning back to look at Patrick.

Patrick went to Greg's apartment the following night. He was intrigued, scared, and curious. He stood outside Greg's apartment door looking up and down the hallway, trying to talk himself out of going through with this meeting. Maybe Greg thinks I have a lot of money, and he thinks I can be blackmailed. He couldn't make much money as a bartender, so he couldn't support my habit. Why was I even standing outside his door? This is stupid. As Patrick was about to walk away, Greg opened his apartment door wearing a terry wrap towel around his waist. His bald head shiny and damp.

Patrick never "went that way" before, but his thinking wasn't clear; his brain was being fried between the drinking and cocaine. Greg grabbed Patrick's arm, pulled him into his apartment and began kissing him. At the same time, he pulled Patrick's hand towards his groin and Patrick pulled away, feeling disgusted. "Sorry man, it's not my thing," he said.

"Then why did you come here?"

"I thought maybe you had some coke I could score."

"Oh, so that's the kind of blow you're looking for. Well, I do have some. And it's very good quality. But before you get that, I want something in return."

"Like I said, man. I don't go that way," Patrick said, backing away and heading towards the front door.

"Well, how about a little snort before you leave. See how you feel then. Maybe you'll change your mind."

Patrick never turned down an offer of drugs. He watched as Greg walked to the kitchen table, and arranged two lines of coke on the glass table.

"Come here," he said to Patrick.

As promised, Greg's coke was incredible. It must have been laced with ecstasy, because Patrick immediately got stoned.

"Ok. I gave you what you wanted. Now it's your turn."

Patrick was hesitant, but something else was controlling his mind. He felt like a cheap prostitute. He remembered what the guys at work called it: gay-for-trade.

Patrick found himself knocking on Greg's door at least once a week. Once he married Casey, he didn't know how he was going to explain his midnight trips. He would worry about that when the time came. Right now, all he cared about was scoring good coke, a great high, and great sex.

But it wasn't too long before Greg started asking for money. Money that Patrick didn't have. He stole from the traders at work, going through their jackets that were hung up in the coat closet, or taking petty cash from their desk drawers. He went through his father's wallet while he was sleeping, and dipped into his mother's purse. His addiction was now costing him his self-respect, and risking his job and future marriage to Casey.

CHAPTER 17

Simone and Jennifer were driving southbound in bumper to bumper traffic on Connecticut's I-95. "I thought by leaving before 8:00 in the morning we would avoid this summer traffic. Who knew that driving thirty miles would take us almost two hours," Simone complained to Jennifer. "I'd like to get to the hotel before 10:00 to make sure the staff sets up the banquet hall according to the floorplan, and then check on Casey before she, or her mother, start bossing the staff around."

Ever since the Bouviers had signed a contract, over a year ago, it was one demand after another from either Casey or her mother.

Simone imitated their conversation:

"'Everything must be perfect,' Casey screamed," Simone said.

"'Yes, everything must be perfect,' her mother echoed like a parrot," Jennifer replied.

"'And if it's not, heads will roll,'" Simone echoed.

"'Yes, roll,' said the parrot," Jennifer said.

"You got that?"

"You got that?"

"Jen, I wanted to give Mrs. Bouvier a cracker"

Jennifer laughed. "You know the staff at the Grand Hamilton are pretty much on target with doing things according to the set-up plans. And don't worry about Casey or Mrs. Bouvier. Casey just wants that ring on her finger so her mother will stop yapping at her about how old she is and not married."

"You're right. I've been on edge for months now about this wedding. Or, maybe it's because we've just come off working those two large events last weekend; I'm exhausted." Simone exited the highway in Greenwich.

"I just can't wait for today's wedding to be over."

Simone and Jennifer had worked numerous high level, stressful weddings together, some that included knife fights, food fights, and a no-show groom. But this wedding was different for Simone, and Jennifer sensed it.

"You seem overly stressed about this wedding, Simone," Jennifer commented. "Anything I need to know?"

"No, nothing," she answered unconvincingly. "Just tired, I guess."

Simone's thoughts traveled to Charlie. Since their exciting night together seven months before, she had avoided any communication with him. He had sent several texts, and left numerous voice mail messages. She responded only once, by text, *Hi. I can't get involved with a married man.* After a few weeks, he got the message she was not interested.

Whenever she worked an event at the Grand Hamilton Hotel, she avoided him, often putting Jennifer in charge. Her pleasantries included a simple, 'hello' but she dodged further conversations. Her guilt took precedence. Charlie deserved an answer. She wasn't angry with him or, surprisingly, with herself. Rather, she was frightened by her longing and desire for him.

It was not Simone's style to have a one-night stand. And she got the feeling it wasn't Charlie's style either. She had dated over the past several years, but no man stayed in her mind like he did. Not since Joe.

Jennifer flipped down the vanity mirror and checked her makeup. She reapplied her bright red lipstick, brushed her long blond hair, and gave herself an approving look.

"I hope her dress fits," Simone said emerging from her daydream. "Jennifer, you should have heard Casey at her final fitting. She was shouting at the seamstress that she screwed up her dress."

"What did the seamstress say?"

"Just like all the other people around Casey, she kowtowed to her. 'Yes, Miss. I'll take it out just a little to make it feel better.' She pulled the same scenario with the other vendors. 'You'd better not screw up my wedding' was her weekly mantra."

Simone was tired of Casey, tired of the bride's mother, and fed up with always having to take care of one emergency or another. This wedding had red flags and flashing lights predicting there was going to be trouble. Simone wasn't feeling good about this wedding.

She came to a halt in front of the dual swinging iron gates, carved with the Gothic letters GHH, leading to the Grand Hamilton Hotel. Once a private estate, it sat on three hundred acres on the élite "Gold Coast" of southwestern Connecticut, situated high on a hill with vistas overlooking Long Island Sound. She shut off the air conditioner, rolled down the windows, and inhaled deeply.

Simone proceeded slowly onto the cobblestone road, taking in the perfectly manicured, lush grounds. "Wow, Jennifer, look at the beautiful flowers this year. I love those pink and violet hydrangeas, and the tiny Lily of the Valley bells. Oh, and look at the peonies."

"Do you smell the lavender?" asked Jennifer.

Simone was reminded of Paris so many years ago.

As she drove slowly to the summit, her heart raced, anxious to see Charlie again.

A loud blast from a car horn snapped both women out of their trance. Simone looked in the rear view mirror while an agitated man made an obscene gesture. "Move it lady," he screamed at her.

"Geez, so much for enjoying nature," Simone growled. She sped up, driving the rest of the way to the entrance. She looked at her watch. It was 10:30am.

Valets, smartly dressed, approached Simone's White Porsche SUV from both sides. After opening the car doors, they extended helping hands to the ladies. They placed everything on a hotel luggage cart, and whisked it off to the vendor's station.

Mother Nature must have heard the bride's screaming threats, because the weather was absolutely perfect. There was a clear blue sky with low humidity, and an on-shore breeze. Not a wind to mess up the bride's hair, but gentle enough to keep her underarms cool during inevitable stressful moments.

But Simone's gut was far from perfect.

Upon stepping past the two large entrance doors, Simone and Jennifer were greeted with, "Welcome to the Grand Hamilton Hotel." They smiled at the attendants, making mental notes that these guys got more attractive each time. One asked, "Are you here for a special event?"

"Yes" Jennifer replied. "We're the planners for the Bouvier/Michaelson wedding." Simone looked around for Charlie, but he wasn't anywhere in sight.

"Very well, ladies. Why don't you check in and get settled. When you're ready, come down to the grand ballroom and ask for Frederick Murphy, the assistant manager."

Weddings at this opulent estate started at $200,000. Single rooms blocked off for a wedding cost $695 a night. Fortunately, the hotel comped rooms for Simone and Jennifer.

Depending on how big a room you reserved, and how much personal service you required, tips are the name of the game at the Grand Hamilton Hotel. Be prepared to come with at least $500 in $5 bills. There were tips for the valets upon arrival, and the delivery of luggage to the room. Tips were required for the personal housekeeper who ironed wrinkled clothing, the personal bartender, the shoe shiner, and the floral and fruit delivery person.

Afterwards, you were $500 poorer, but looked like a million bucks.

"I'll meet you in the lobby in fifteen minutes," Simone said as Jennifer got off the elevator.

Usually, Simone and Jennifer were given one large room with two queen beds. But today, they were given two separate rooms. Jennifer's ample room was on the Concierge Level. Simone's room was on the Executive floor.

Simone's room housed a large king-size bed, a sitting room, an efficiency kitchen, and a bathroom almost the size of Simone's own living room. She knew why she was given such a room - Charlie Hamilton.

Simone changed from jeans into her standard work outfit consisting of a white Oxford-style shirt, black slacks and soft black shoes. Across her chest was her leather messenger bag containing day-of related paperwork. She knew Jennifer would be wearing a short dress flattering her perfect figure, and 6" Ferragamo heels.

The two women met at the elevator banks, waiting for the banquet manager in charge that day. Simone secretly hoped it wasn't Charlie.

"Hello. I'm Frederick, the assistant banquet manager," came a booming voice from behind them, startling both women. Simone looked up at the towering man with cold, piercing blue eyes and extended a hand, but all she got in return was, "Right this way." Simone had seen Frederick working as wait staff, but not in his role as banquet manager.

He looked more like a military man in his finely pressed gray uniform, as he took lengthy strides heading towards the grand ballroom. Simone and Jennifer quickened their pace to keep up with him. He pushed open the large double doors, which clicked shut behind them.

"The vendor's work station is beyond on the right. Have you worked a wedding here before? Do you know the house rules?"

Jennifer opened her mouth to speak, but only a "we" was spoken before Frederick took two steps forward, turned on his heels, faced them, and snapped, "The vendors - that would be you," he said pointing at them, "are not allowed to partake in alcohol, talking to the guests, or eating, until all the guests have been seated and served their food. After that, you will be served sandwiches and soda in the vendor's room. You are not to eat any passed hors d'oeuvres or stand within ten feet of the open bars." Suddenly, Simone felt the urge to smack him.

"We've worked several events at the Hamilton," Jennifer answered. She wanted to add, "You've seen us here before," but was cut off with, "The GRAND Hamilton," he sternly corrected her.

"Yep, the GRAND Hamilton," Jennifer said flippantly. Frederick abruptly turned and left the banquet hall, leaving the ladies standing there with their mouths agape.

CHAPTER 18

"What a creep," Simone said, annoyed by his attitude.

Jennifer nodded. "A frustrated nerd."

They looked around the Grand Ballroom and took mental inventory of what needed to be done. The ceremony was at 6:00 with the reception immediately following. Everything must be set up to the Bouvier's requests, and double checked by 5:30.

Fortunately, Simone's two assistants, Katy and Jonathan, arrived early and were in the middle of reviewing the floorplan with the head of the kitchen staff.

"Hi Katy," Simone interrupted, leaving Jonathan to focus on the details. "Jennifer and I will do a quick review of what's been set up already, and then head up to work with the bride. We'll be back in an hour or so. If you need anything, just text me."

"Good luck, Simone," Katy said. "Casey and her mother were already down here bossing the staff. Our contact person, Frederick, encouraged them to go back to their rooms. I think he scared them." Simone chuckled at the thought.

Casey-Ann Bouvier was a classic Bridezilla. Her mother, Amanda Bouvier was a Motherzilla. She didn't think twice about calling Simone at any hour of the day or night for a 'quick question,' which seemed to turn into a half hour conversation. Simone remembered one of her favorites:

"Did you talk to the printer about the invitations? How about the florist? Did she order the orchids from Hawaii?"

"Yes, Mrs. Bouvier. I spoke to them the other day and emailed you a confirmation. The invitations will be printed this week, and the orchids have been ordered."

"Well, I don't trust emails. Maybe someone hacked into your account and sent me an email as a joke."

"No, Mrs. Bouvier. No one has hacked into my computer system. No one's joking around here."

"You know everything has to be perfect."

"Yes, Mrs. Bouvier. Everything will be top-notch."

"Or else, heads will roll."

"Yes, Mrs. Bouvier. Heads will roll."

"Do you know if Mrs. Michaelson has her dress?" asked Simone.

"How would I know? I don't talk to that woman."

Simone didn't want to open that can of worms. "I'll call her later this week and check in."

"Well, she had better have her dress. And make sure it's not blue. Or short. Or sleeveless. I'm wearing blue. And my arms are too fat to wear sleeveless, so she better not think she can show off her emaciated arms by wearing sleeveless."

"Yes, Mrs. Bouvier. Have a good evening, Mrs. Bouvier. I have another call coming in. I'll check in with you later this week."

Whenever Simone saw Mrs. Bouvier's number on her Caller ID, she let the call go to voicemail. Casey and her mother were two of the most difficult and entitled people she and Jennifer had worked with in a long time.

The planners had spent countless days with Casey and her mother, shopping for a wedding gown, and the mother-of-the bride dress, and picking out invitations, favors, and flowers. They attended food and wine tastings, contract negotiation sessions, and numerous band showcases. Simone and her staff worked endless hours on the guest list, RSVP cards, seating cards and charts, the overall floor plan, reviewing and confirming vendor contracts. Lots of time was spent figuring out who couldn't sit with certain people because of bad blood.

At one of the seating-plan meetings, Mrs. Bouvier told Simone and Jennifer, "Sophia can't be sitting with, or near Carlos. You know they had an affair a few years ago, and Sophia's husband carries a gun. We don't want anyone shot at Casey's wedding. They can shoot each other later."

"No, Mrs. Bouvier, Sophia won't be sitting with Carlos. But I can't guarantee the two families won't meet at the carving station." Simone winked at Jennifer.

"Carving station. Oh my, Simone," Mrs. Bouvier said, her anxiety moving up a few notches. "We can't have that. Make sure you're at the carving station the whole time. You, too, Jennifer. Make sure Sophia and her husband don't see Carlos."

"Yes, Mrs. Bouvier. We'll stand by the carving station watching Sophia. We'll make sure she doesn't make goo-goo eyes at Carlos."

"Simone, don't joke around. This is very serious," snapped Mrs. Bouvier. "If you see Sophia near Carlos, or if you see them giving each other the come-hither look, tell Mr. Bouvier."

"Yes, Mrs. Bouvier. We'll make sure there aren't any goo-goo eyes at Casey's wedding."

"Good."

On the drive back from the meeting, the women howled with laughter.

"Jennifer, we can't make this stuff up. No one would believe what we have to put up with planning weddings.

"Isn't it amazing, Jen, when we met the Bouviers she seemed so reserved – almost nervous. Now, she's barking orders."

"When she's around her husband, she plays the reserved little wife. But when he's away, the beast comes out," added Jennifer.

When planners get paid well for jobs like this one, and work in beautiful settings like the Grand Hamilton Hotel, blind eyes and deaf ears are turned to such outbursts by brides and their mothers. Simone trained herself to blame a client's insults, screaming and demands on wedding day jitters, and wedding planning stress. Conversely, on the wedding day, the bride and her mother can't praise Simone and her staff enough, with kisses, hugs and accolades that often make Simone nauseated.

The grand ballroom had thirty-six round tables set up around the room, as well as a dais for the bridal party. The tables were adorned with simple and elegant pale yellow overlays on top of white cotton tablecloths. Capiz shells of pearly iridescence were used as chargers, giving the tables a level of elegance.

After all the tables were set, Katy and Jonathan checked each table, making certain they had the correct number of place settings, all the dishes and utensils were free from lipstick, cracks, stains or dried-on food. No matter where a wedding took place, from the Grand Hamilton Hotel to a church hall, an errant coffee cup with a red lipstick stain always made its way to a place setting.

Just as Simone and Jennifer were looking over the floorplan, the florist's van arrived. The delivery boy unloaded dozens of huge floral arrangements, the bride's orchid bouquet, and bridal party bouquets, corsages for the mothers, a grandmother, and two aunts. Jennifer counted the delivery, matching it to the contract.

"We're short five boutonnieres," she told the pimply-faced delivery boy.

"What's a booton-air? he asked.

"The flower a man wears on his lapel."

Everyone involved was working with a tight time schedule, and the last thing they needed was a major delay.

"Call your boss," Jennifer told the boy. "Tell her she's short five 'booton-airs.' She'll know what you're talking about."

"Sorry, Miss. I ain't allowed to use a cell phone no more while I'm at work."

Jennifer took in a deep breath.

"Tell your boss that I gave you permission to use your cell phone while you're on the job. If she has a problem with that, tell her to call me."

Simone watched as he took out a cell phone from his back pocket, a business card from another pocket, and called his boss.

"I have to go back to the shop. I'll be back in a few minutes," the pimply kid announced to no one in particular.

Simone and Jennifer went back to the floorplan and checked the list. They inspected the carefully ironed tablecloths and napkins as they were being placed on the tables. They looked perfect, and the bride shouldn't have any complaints.

"I don't want to see any folds or wrinkles on my tablecloths," the bride had shrieked at the assistant manager at one of their planning meetings.

"Yes, Miss. We'll be sure to press all the tablecloths and napkins to your satisfaction." He must have been used to dealing with women like Casey as her demand didn't seem to faze him in the least.

Simone and Jennifer headed up to the bridal suite, leaving Katy and Jonathan to oversee the rest of the banquet hall for dirty napkins tossed under side tables, fingerprints on mirrors, water stains on glasses, broken chairs, and spider webs. Then, they perused the oversized bathrooms, with more accoutrements than those at the Ritz.

It is rare to find such problems at five-star hotels like the Grand Hamilton Hotel, The Ritz, or The Four Seasons. But sometimes, a renegade toothpick lodges itself between the rug and wall.

CHAPTER 19

At noon, Simone and Jennifer arrived at the bridal suite to find Casey Bouvier sitting on the edge of her bed in tears.

"Oh no," Simone whispered to Jennifer. "Look at this place. It's as if a hurricane came through."

Simone looked around. Strewn over every surface of the room were wet towels, underwear, jeans, tee shirts, shoes, open suitcases, trays of half eaten food, and empty wine bottles.

"Hey, Casey, what's going on?" Simone said, feigning a nonchalant stance. She learned that the more you feed into the drama, the bigger it gets.

"My life is over," Casey cried. "Can't you see that I look horrible in this dress, my eyes are puffy, my stomach is protruding, and my hair is a mess?"

"Where's your stylist? Isn't she supposed to be helping you get dressed?"

"I fired her - she's an incompetent idiot. All she keeps talking about is her stupid Hungarian tea. It's going to help me make babies. I don't want a baby," she sobbed.

Simone turned to Jennifer, who still had their workbag hanging on her shoulder. "Can you take out the water and eye cream?"

While Jennifer took out the necessary items, Simone grabbed a bunch of tissues and handed them to Casey. "Blow your nose, and wipe your tears. Tell me what's going on."

"Everybody is telling me what to do," Casey said in between sniffs. "My mother, my bridesmaids, that stupid stylist . . . everybody. I hate them all," she said as she gave her nose a final blow and handed the dirty tissues to Simone.

Jennifer handed Simone the eye cream. "Casey, put some of this cream under your eyes. This might sting a little, but it goes away quickly. This will diffuse the puffiness."

Casey starred at the tube of Preparation H. "I'm not putting ass cream on my face," she yelled, flaying her arms at Simone. "Get that away from me."

"Really? Do you want everyone to say, 'Oh, doesn't she look puffy and old?' If not, put this under your eyes," Simone said with determination. Tell a woman that she'll make an ugly bride, and she'll hang on to your every word to make herself look pretty.

Casey finally acquiesced and dabbed a bit of the 'miracle gel' under her bloodshot blue eyes. Jennifer handed Simone two bottles of Evian, and placed an additional three bottles on her makeup table.

"I want you to drink a lot of water, so that you can pee away some of the puffiness." Casey obeyed and began sipping the water.

"Where's your mother?" Jennifer asked.

"I told that old bag to get out of my face. I have no idea where she is. This is my wedding, not hers. The meddling old bitch. From the minute I got engaged she's been ordering me around, telling me that I have to invite this-one and that-one, the food I have to serve, what kind of dress . . . she even wanted to write my vows."

"Casey, I'd like you to sit here for a few minutes, take some deep breaths and keep drinking the water. Let the Preparation H do its thing. I bet you didn't have anything to eat today." Casey shook her head 'no'.

Simone picked up the hotel phone and asked for Room Service. She focused on her partner, and whispered, "Jennifer, please find Hilda. Beg her to come back and help Casey with her hair and makeup. Offer her more money if necessary, but get Hilda here. If she's gone home, call one of the other stylists working with the bridal party. After you get a stylist, check on Mrs. Bouvier and the bridesmaids. Make sure they're dressed and ready for the photographer, who will be here at 3:00."

Jennifer left on her mission. Simone watched Casey, and had a feeling that something other than wedding jitters was going on with her.

"Room Service. Sorry to keep you holding," snapped Simone back into the moment. She placed a breakfast order for Casey, asking it to be delivered as quickly as possible.

Casey swayed as she walked back and forth from the dressing table to the toilet, and back again.

Simone picked up wet towels and tossed them onto the bathroom floor.

Jennifer returned. "Simone, Mrs. Bouvier isn't answering her room phone or cell phone. I'll go to her room and try to talk to her. Hilda is on her way back to assist with Casey's hair and makeup."

"I don't want to see that monster. She doesn't know what she's doing," Casey screamed from the toilet, with her dress up around her waist and the door open.

"Who?" Simone asked.

"Hilda. She's a witch. And my mother. I hate them both."

"Where are your bridesmaids? I thought they'd be here helping you get ready."

"I told them to go to hell. They're just stupid little twats who started ordering me around."

Simone wondered if the bridesmaids were reprimanding Casey because they were seeing what she and Jennifer saw: a woman, about to get married, who was either stoned or drunk. Or both.

Casey came out of the bathroom, sat on her bed, and started crying.

Simone sat down next to her. "Take slow, deep breaths Casey. If you don't want Hilda, your mother, or your bridesmaids here, how about I style your hair? First I'd cut off that blond bird's nest sitting on your head."

"Those are my extensions," she howled.

"Casey, calm down and listen to us."

She hesitated for a few moments. "Okay," she said, and began to cry again.

"Casey, stop crying. You've got butt cream on your face."

She looked at Simone and began to laugh hysterically. Rivers of black mascara circumvented around the Preparation H as they streaked down her face. She had now switched from anger, to laughter and back to tears. She had become histrionic and out of control.

Simone walked into Casey's bathroom and found the culprits: bottles of Xanax and Valium, and a glass of red wine, a red lipstick stain on the rim. Simone held them up and showed Jennifer, who shook her head in disbelief.

Suddenly, there was a knock at the door. It was Hilda, a short and rotund woman in her late 60s, with white hair and a matching-colored uniform. She resembled a snowman. She waddled over to Casey, who was still sitting on the edge of her bed.

She knelt down beside her and in a heavy Hungarian accent said, "Casey, my darling. I so sorry I upset you. Please, forgive me. Let me help you. You look the prettiest bride ever."

Simone and Jennifer looked at each other, and rolled their eyes.

"Oh Hilda," Casey said between tears, "thank you for coming back. I forgive you."

Hilda removed the hairpins from Casey's hair and looked at her face. "Who put this cream on your face, my darling?"

"She did," sniffled Casey, pointed a trembling, wicked-witch finger at Simone. Simone waited for a reprimand.

"Wonderful," Hilda said. "It works beautiful. You look beautiful, my darling. A beautiful bride. Now, take off your dress and go wash your face. We start again. Okay? I make you some tea to calm your nerves. Old Hungarian tea. Good for bride. Help you make babies tonight."

Simone waited for the screaming to begin. Nothing. Casey nodded her head as if in a zombie state. The Xanax and Valium were kicking in. She stood up, turned her back to Hilda, who unzipped her wedding dress. Casey stepped out of it, and prodded towards the bathroom. All she had on was a garter belt with white lace stockings, and a blue garter around her thigh.

Hilda picked up the hotel phone, "Please bring up large pot of hot water and one of your fancy china teacup for my bride. Bridal Suite One. Yes, bring with breakfast food. Thank you."

"We're leaving now, Casey," Simone announced as they headed toward the door. "We'll be back later before the photographer gets here at 3:00. You can find us in the banquet hall if you need us. And be sure to eat some breakfast."

"I help Casey," Hilda whispered. "I make sure she eat, and drink tea. She look beautiful. You come back later and see."

"Thank you Hilda," Simone whispered. "You've saved the day." Simone gave her a hug.

Hilda smiled and said, "I work with brides like Casey all the time. I know. She nervous. No worry. She be ready in time for pictures."

"Be sure there aren't any wrinkles in the tablecloths," Casey yelled from the bathroom, while she dried her face.

"No wrinkles, Casey. We'll make sure."

Simone and Jennifer left Casey in Hilda's capable hands. As they waited for the elevator, Jennifer joked, "I wonder what sort of tea she's going to make for Casey. Maybe we should get a case of it for our other brides."

CHAPTER 20

It was 12:45 when the women left Casey and Hilda.

At Hilda's coaxing, Casey put on the thick terrycloth hotel robe. "You don't want room service boy to see you with no clothes."

Hilda went to work, putting Casey's hair back into place. She combed out the curls and maneuvered her hair into a chignon, pulled tightly behind her head.

"You look so beautiful, my darling. Your hair off your back, show off your dress." Hilda started to apply fresh makeup on Casey's face.

There was a knock at the door. Hilda opened it while Casey admired herself in the mirror. The room service attendant pushed a cart hosting a silver teapot of boiling water, a fancy teacup on a saucer, and a cloche over a dish of scrambled eggs and toast.

"Thank you, young man," said Hilda.

The attendant stood behind Casey, waiting for the receipt signature. He stared at Casey through the mirror. *The rich bitch is still beautiful, just as I remember,* he thought. *Of all the hotels, she had to have her wedding here. She always did things to torture me, and today isn't any different.*

Casey lifted her head and looked through the mirror at the man in uniform. They locked eyes. Something about him seemed familiar, and a slight hint of recognition showed in her eyes.

Hilda broke the moment by handing the attendant the receipt. He took it, and left the room.

Hilda placed the breakfast in front of Casey. "Eat, my darling."

She rolled the cart into the bathroom, and prepared her special Hungarian tea.

Meanwhile, Casey forced herself to eat some of the eggs. But after a few bites, she put the cloche over the dish.

While the tea was brewing, Hilda helped Casey get back into her dress, and turned her toward the mirror.

"Oh, so beautiful you look," exclaimed Hilda.

After the tea was brewed, Hilda carefully balanced the cup on its saucer, making sure not to spill any of the special concoction.

"Casey, sit down, and now you drink special tea. Only less than two hours before you take pictures, and later you be new wife. This tea relax you."

Casey brought the cup up to her lips. Her nasal passages constricted at the smell. The bitter tea stung her tongue, and she started to gag. Casey spit the tea back into the teacup, and ran to the toilet where she forced herself to throw up.

"Bitch," Hilda said under breath. While Casey was retching, Hilda took the cup to the bathroom sink and threw out the rest of the tea. She wiped the cup and saucer with a hotel hand towel. She put the remaining tea leaves, cup, saucer and towel into her pocketbook.

"I sorry you don't like tea. Your stomach too nervous. I go check your mommy to see if she is dressed. You rest."

CHAPTER 21

Casey Bouvier sat at her dressing table admiring herself in the mirror. "I never thought this day would come. I really am a beautiful bride," she said aloud.

There was a knock at the door. "Coming," Casey shouted. But it opened before she could rise from her chair.

Casey turned her head and stared at the familiar face.

"Hi Casey. I've come to wish you good luck before your wedding." The visitor closed the door.

"Thank you. But you could have wished me luck at the wedding."

"Yes, I know. But I also want to give you a special wedding gift, privately, that I know you will appreciate."

"How did you get in without a key? And what are you doing in that uniform?" Casey asked, trying to conceal the unexpected excitement rising inside her. "If you've come to discuss what happened between us, I'm sorry it didn't work out."

The caller stood behind Casey as she sat in the chair facing the mirror. "You look beautiful in this strapless gown, you know. Just as I imagined you would."

"You're making me feel uncomfortable."

"Am I, now? Uncomfortable or excited?" The visitor began kissing her bare neck and shoulders. "You know you are marrying Patrick simply because his family has money. You didn't want to be with me because I lacked money and position."

"Don't be ridiculous. I'm marrying Patrick because I love him." Casey closed her eyes, as an ancient ache began to stir for this former lover. Her breathing accelerated. A faint sexual moan rose in her throat. This was a passionate lover, willing to explore past the norm. Patrick was boring, and a weakling. She was slowly losing control.

"You said you loved me, too."

She opened her eyes and stared at the familiar face through the mirror. She whispered, "I'm sorry, I really am. Truth be told, I did love you. But I'm afraid of being poor. I was afraid mummy and daddy would cut me off if I was with you."

The kissing abruptly stopped. "Stop this pretentious shit, Casey. Mummy and daddy. When did you become so righteous? You never introduced me to your parents for fear they'd throw you out of the house. You dumped me because of my injury. We were no longer the secret lovers on campus. You just moved on to the next person who could satisfy your desires."

Casey spun around in her seat. Correct on all points, but she'd never admit it. She stood up and begged, "Make love to me. Right now. Just one more time."

The former lover's eyes filled with desire. "My how your mind twists and turns so quickly. I'd make love to you in an instant Casey, you know that. But, I don't think my scent should be on you. Not on your wedding day. Like I said, I just wanted to stop by to wish you luck and give you a gift."

The visitor handed Casey a small black box, tied with a white silk ribbon. With trembling hands, she slowly untied the ribbon, letting it fall to the floor. Inside, wrapped in tissue paper, was a small glass vile of cocaine.

"I remember how much you love this stuff."

Casey stared at the gift. Her eyes widened and a smile spread across her face. "Oh my! Just what I need. Thank you. This is the best gift anyone could give me."

Casey watched as the gift was presented to her on the glass top of her dressing table. "None for you?"

"I had some already. That is how I got the courage to come and see you."

She bent over the precious white powder and snorted the two thin lines. She sat up and smiled at her guest.

"Thank you. This blow is great."

"My pleasure. Only the best for you, my love."

Casey's reaction was immediate. Her pupils began dilating, and she found it difficult to speak. She was flying high. Her heart raced uncontrollably. Her chest felt constricted, stifling her breathing. Rasping sounds projected from her mouth. A small stream of blood trickled from her nose, staining her white Vera Wang gown, followed by tears smearing through her professionally-applied makeup.

As the door to Casey's room closed, she gurgled, "Why?"

"Because you broke my heart."

"But I still love you."

CHAPTER 22

As they rode the elevator down to the lobby, Simone said, "Let's check in with Katy and Jonathan. Afterwards, I'll get the hotel doctor's number, and you can check on Mrs. Bouvier. If you have time, check in with Patrick. I suspect he is a coke-head, and will be as stoned as Casey."

"Funny you should say that, Simone. I was thinking the same thing about Patrick."

They reviewed the set-up in the Grand Ballroom with Katy and Jonathan. Feeling satisfied that things were on schedule, and in good hands, Simone and Jennifer agreed to meet back in Casey's room at 1:45.

Simone went off to face her fears: Charlie.

Simone met "I'm-more-important-than-you-Frederick" as she was walking down the thickly carpeted hallway. His name tag should read "Frankenstein", she thought.

"Can I help you?" he asked Simone. He had a stern look on his fair colored face and tried using his 6'6" intimidating height to tower over Simone's tiny 5'1" frame.

"I have to see Charlie. Is he in his office?"

"Do you mean Mr. Charles Hamilton? What's this about? He can't be disturbed. I'm sure I can handle any questions you might have."

"It's a personal matter that only Charlie can handle." She walked quickly away from him.

"Let me escort you to his office." Perfectly timed, a hotel staff member approached Frederick with a question.

Whew, saved by the bellhop, she thought. Simone strode off waving her hand in the air. "I know where his office is. Thanks anyway."

Charlie's grandfather, Charles Hamilton IV, lived in this mansion before it was turned into a banquet facility back in the 1990s. His father,

Charles Hamilton V, was instrumental with the design and upgrades to the property, and he oversaw the corporate operations.

By inherited rights, Charlie, the sixth Hamilton, should be in charge. But, he was considered a failure by his grandfather and father. Charlie and his wife had never produced an heir, a son, a Charles Hamilton VII. Charlie's wife was more interested in producing a name for herself.

Most likely, the property would be left to Charlie's sister, Harriet, and her husband. They had six kids, four of them boys.

Simone took a deep breath, and nervously knocked on the door. "Come in."

Simone slowly opened the office door. Charlie was sitting with his feet up on his desk watching a baseball game on a large flat screen TV.

"Hi, Charlie."

"Oh my God, Simone." He swung his legs off his desk as he clicked off the TV. "I saw on the work sheets that you were the planner for the Bouvier wedding. When did you arrive? I wanted to welcome you. How are you? Do you need any help with your bags? Do you like your room?" The rapid barrage of questions continued. He rushed around his desk, wrapping his arms around Simone in a bear hug. After a few uncomfortable moments, she pulled away, feeling her face growing warm.

"Thanks for the suite, Charlie. It's gorgeous. Frederick welcomed us and read us the riot act. You've got to promote your staff, they're so frustrated having these menial jobs."

He stared at her, "Simone, I think about you all the time. Why won't you return my phone calls or texts? I miss you so much."

She raised a hand motioning him to stop before he said anything else. But her STOP sign, didn't work. "Please come work here. Be by my side. You're one of the best wedding planners on the east coast. We can go far together," Charlie said.

"Don't flatter me. Sometimes, I detest the entitled brides, and wish they were all dead. And you know as well as I do, we could never work together, no less be together. You're married." How could she tell Charlie that she secretly wanted to be with him, too? She thought about him often, reliving the evening they had spent together.

He lowered his head. "I'm separated from my wife, Simone. She served me with divorce papers last Christmas." He paused. "She asked me to leave the house. I'm now living here at the hotel. I don't have a life. She wants everything . . . the house, part of the business, the boat, and the cars . . . all of it. She's tired of me working all the time. Hell, I didn't have a life before, and I certainly don't have one now."

"Did she find out about our evening together?"

"No. Although, someone told her we had dinner together. She stayed at her parents' that Thanksgiving weekend, so she didn't know what I was doing. She says I'm not home enough and she doesn't want to be tied down any longer. She complains that she has to go to all the social events alone. I think she's having an affair with the tennis pro. Honestly, I really don't care. Our marriage was over years ago. It's just difficult going through all the legal steps." Then changing the subject, he said, "Spend the night with me, Simone," he begged. "No one needs to know."

"I can't Charlie. It's unprofessional. I don't want Jennifer finding out. I never told her about us, and I don't want to start now. I think she's a little suspicious. Besides, Jennifer and I need to leave here early tomorrow morning. We're flying out to Los Angeles for a big wedding next weekend."

She changed the subject. "Charlie, I need the name and number of the hotel doctor. I think we've got a bride addicted to pain killers. I found bottles of Xanax and Valium in Casey Bouvier's bathroom, and a few empty bottles of wine. She's acting irrational . . . simultaneously crying and laughing. She fired her hairstylist, threw her maid-of-honor and her mother out of the room. Her eyes look 'glassy,' and I'm concerned she's going to pass out while walking down the aisle. I'd like to have the doctor in attendance during the ceremony."

"Sure. Anything you want." He paused and stared at her. "Can I at least kiss you, Simone? Please."

Simone's heart pounded.

She feared she would lose control if he kissed her. But she wanted him to hold her in his arms, to kiss her, to make love to her that instant.

Charlie's deep brown puppy eyes pulled on Simone's heart strings.

He moved in closer to Simone. He gently took her face in his firm hands and leaned in. He paused for a second and they stared at each other. She could feel his warm breath on her face. He tilted his head and their lips gently touched.

The office door burst open. It was Frederick. "Mr. Hamilton, we have an emergency."

"Don't you know how to knock?" snapped Charlie, as he quickly backed away from Simone.

"Sorry, sir," he said, realizing the intrusion.

Frederick looked at Simone. "You are needed in the bridal suite immediately. Miss Bouvier is dead."

CHAPTER 23

"This can't be happening," Simone said, as the three of them bolted out of Charlie's office.

"Frederick, did Jennifer say what happened?" Charlie asked.

"No, sir. She just called the operator to say the bride passed out and to get the EMS. I heard the call on my walkie." Frederick tapped the Bluetooth device nestled in his ear. Something nagged at Simone, but her body was high on adrenaline, and she couldn't focus on that now. "I ran up to the room and Jennifer was doing CPR on Miss Bouvier. She screamed, 'Find Simone.'"

Since the Grand Hamilton was a huge estate, they had their own staff physician, EMS, an ambulance, and three security officers, one of them always on duty. The closest hospital was twenty minutes away, which was too far for those who needed immediate attention.

The three arrived at the bridal suite. The bride's parents, the groom, and his parents ran down the hallway, heading to Casey's room. The doctor and the hotel security officer had already arrived.

Casey's parents, visibly shaken, were crying. Mrs. Bouvier's head was buried in her husband's chest, his white tuxedo shirt stained with black mascara and beige makeup. Patrick was sniffling. The future in-laws stood by, gaping in horror.

Jennifer sat in the corner of the room, her head resting on her bent knees. Her spike heels were tossed a few feet away, the red soles resembling the color of blood stains on the beige carpet.

She looked up at Simone with tear-filled eyes and patted the floor next to her. Simone sat down and put her arm around Jennifer's shoulders.

"What happened?"

"It was awful, Simone."

While the police asked questions of Casey's parents and the groom, Jennifer explained to Simone the course of events. "After you and I left the Grand Ballroom, I went to Mrs. Bouvier's suite. Casey's maid-of-honor was there, as well. They reported that Casey was yelling and screaming at them and at Hilda, to get out of her room. Casey didn't want them at her wedding.

"Mrs. Bouvier was crying, saying, 'something is wrong with my daughter.' I assured her that it was normal for the bride to be nervous, and not to take her insults personally. I said I would check on Casey and everything would be fine, and for them to get ready in time for the photographer at 3:00."

Jennifer continued, "Simone, we saw how Casey was acting . . . her yelling, unsteady gait, crying, and laughing. It must have devastated her mother. When I got here, I found Casey sitting at her dressing table. I asked if she was alright, and she didn't answer. I waved my hand in front of her face, and her eyes were blank. I poked her arm and she fell over. I called the operator, and asked for the doctor. Then, I checked for a pulse, and she didn't have one. So I began CPR. Frederick arrived, and I told him to find you."

Simone placed her arm around her partner's shoulder, as Jennifer broke into another round of tears. She handed her some tissues, and a bottle of water from their work bag sitting nearby. Simone looked at her friend and partner, and quipped, "You need some 'butt cream,' girlfriend."

Jennifer omitted a forced laugh. "I need a drink more than that."

Simone walked over to the dresser to grab a bottle of wine. As her hand was about to circle the neck of a bottle, a hand closed around her wrist.

Charlie intervened. "Don't touch anything," he said in a low voice, "until they know the cause of death. No one should even be in this room."

His touch shot through her, initiating a new level of arousal.

Simone whispered, "Charlie, it'll be okay. She probably died of a drug overdose, combined with wine, and who-knows-what-else."

"I have to protect the hotel and the guests," he softly countered. He paused a few moments, then stared at her face, which was devoid of emotion. "You don't seem to be very upset by any of this."

"I'm a tough woman, Charlie. I've been trained to work through emergencies, and fall apart later. No one gets past my protective wall. To answer your question earlier, that is why I never returned your calls after our evening together. You were crossing my line of defense."

He stared at Simone, with a look he couldn't decipher. Was it anger, passion, pity or desperation?

She softened, "Charlie, you know I'm here. I'll help you through this."

They stood only inches apart, whispering, with his hand still holding her wrist. Realizing this, Simone stepped back. Her eyes darted to her wrist and back at Charlie. He released his grip. She was concerned that others would notice their intense connection.

Two Greenwich Police Officers arrived to take over for the hotel security officer. A police photographer, along with an investigative team, followed behind. Over the cacophony of the radios, the officer in charge, announced, "We need everyone to leave. We need to close off this room immediately and begin our investigation."

Other hotel guests standing in the hallway speculated with each other, wondering what had happened. Frederick gave them an update. Charlie noticed him talking to the guests and quickly left the room to deflect any gossip from spreading through the hotel.

"Frederick, thank you for comforting the guests," Charlie said, "but you are needed back in the bridal suite." Frederick gave him a quizzical look, but obliged. Charlie turned to the guests, "Unfortunately, the bride has taken ill. Everything is under control. We're sorry for any inconvenience. Please return to what you were doing. The police need the hallway cleared. Thank you." Charlie turned and walked away from the waiting crowd and toward the bridal suite.

"What do you think you were doing, Frederick?" Charlie reprimanded him. "It is no one's business what goes on in this hotel. By giving them information, they'll think there's a murderer running around here.

Never inform the guests as to what is happening, unless you receive direct orders from me. Is that understood?"

"Yes, sir."

"Are you the parents of the bride?" the police officer asked, as he approached the Bouviers.

They nodded in unison. "Yes. We are Bruce and Amanda Bouvier. Our daughter, Casey, was to be married today . . ." Mrs. Bouvier's voice trailed off, as she continued sobbing.

"I'm sorry for your loss. I need you to go back to your room. Officer Jones will follow you to your suite, where he'll take your statements." He looked around and saw another tuxedo-clad man, sitting in a side chair, looking dazed. "Are you the groom?"

"Yeah," Patrick responded between sniffles.

"May I have your name please?"

"Michaelson. Patrick Michaelson. And these are my parents."

"Please follow Officer Jones to Mr. and Mrs. Bouvier's room. We'll need to get your statement, as well. We are sorry for your loss."

He turned and looked at Charlie, Frederick, Jennifer and Simone. "I'm sorry to say that everyone who was working with the victim is considered a suspect. No one can leave the hotel until we get your statements," he said, looking at Jennifer and Simone. "And from you, too, Mr. Hamilton. I believe there was also an assistant manager who saw the victim?"

"Yes, that's me," Frederick said, standing from just outside the suite. "Frederick Murphy, sir."

"Mr. Hamilton, can you arrange for a conference room to be available? I'd like to get statements from the four of you." He looked at his watch and said, "Is 3:00 ok?"

"Yes, certainly. We will meet in Room 106 at 3:00."

A police photographer started taking photos of the room. The hotel security officer picked up the white ribbon and empty black box from the floor, and placed it on the dressing table.

"Don't touch anything in the room," the police photographer instructed.

"Oh sorry, I thought I was helping," replied the security officer.

The photographer continued the reprimand, "You need to be wearing gloves. You should know better than to touch anything at a crime scene."

"A crime scene? I thought she died of a drug overdose."

The officer looked at him. "What makes you think that?"

"I just overheard the girls talking."

"We won't know until the autopsy is performed. Everything inside the room: glasses, clothes, bedding, and bottles are to be removed and sent to the crime lab."

"May I take my workbag?" Simone asked as she walked towards it, interrupting the tension-filled conversation between the hotel security officer and the police photographer.

"Sorry ma'am, it is considered evidence, and will be taken to the crime lab for analysis," a voice boomed from behind her. His name plate read, McGUIRE.

"How long before I can get it back?"

"It could take a few weeks, ma'am. I don't know."

"A few weeks? But that's my business," Simone interrupted.

"Sorry ma'am. I can't help you."

Simone was concerned about losing a work bag, because a replacement cost several hundred dollars. The workbag was her constant companion at every event. It is a large, army-green canvas bag with a sturdy brass zipper and sturdy shoulder straps. It was packed with numerous essentials, often needed on the day of an event. Among the basics, were household tools, a first aid kit, Tide To Go sticks, Preparation H, Kaopectate, smelling salts, breath mints, a rescue inhaler, a meditation book, a selection of Harlequin romance novels, condoms, and pilfered Viagra pills.

A percentage of items are lost at every event. Either the bartenders can't find wine bottle openers, which aren't returned, or the DJ shows up short an extension cord and/or power strip.

Fortunately, the most important documents for that day were inside Simone's messenger bag that she wore across her chest. It contained contracts with the client and vendors, copies of emails, the guest list, correspondence, and layout designs of the venue. If she lost that, she'd be in big trouble.

Officer McGuire announced, "We're closing off this room now. Everyone please leave."

Simone, Jennifer and Charlie followed Casey's parents as they made their way to the elevators. "Mr. and Mrs. Bouvier," Simone said as she caught up to them, "I'm terribly sorry for your loss. I know this isn't the best time, but I think we should all meet to discuss our next steps."

"If there's anything the hotel can do for you, please let me know," added Charlie.

"You want your money, don't you," Mr. Bouvier suddenly snapped. Mrs. Bouvier stood by rubbing her pearls, occasionally dabbing at her eyes with a tissue, and pushing her eyeglasses back into place.

This statement took Simone by surprise. The topic of money was far from her mind. "That is not what I'm saying, sir. Not at all. I'd like to discuss how you wish to proceed. Mr. Bouvier, please ask your son to join us; Patrick too. Some decisions need to be made. Mr. Hamilton can arrange a conference room, I'm sure."

"It's now 2:50," Simone said looking at her watch. "Jennifer and I have to give statements to the police in a few minutes. Can we meet you downstairs at 4:00? Mr. Hamilton will post the conference room number on the hotel's information screen."

"Okay, but if there's any mention of money, I'll sue all of you," Mr. Bouvier snapped. He turned away from them, put his arm under his wife's elbow while saying, "Come along, Mother," and escorted her into the elevator, followed by Patrick and his parents, and Officer Jones.

Once the elevator doors closed, Simone turned to her partner, "Jennifer, please call Katy and Jonathan. Inform them of what has happened, and that the four of us need to meet in the banquet hall at 3:30. We should be finished with the police by then. Ask them to stop doing whatever it is they're working on right now, and to notify the kitchen staff to wait for further instructions from Charlie."

She turned to Charlie, "I'm assuming that Frederick can take over for you regarding any evening activities relating to the Bouviers?"

"I'm not sure, given he had some contact with Casey. When I talk to my father, I'll tell him to send over one of the other banquet managers to work with Frederick. What are you thinking, Simone?" Charlie asked.

"After Jennifer and I meet with our staff, I'll fill you in. I'll see you in the conference room with the police in a few minutes."

It was situations like this that made Simone one of the most sought after wedding planners in the area. She knew what needed to be done in an emergency. She thought creatively, and took charge. At one wedding a few years back, the caterer had erroneously booked the event for the following day. "There's no way I can get food for one hundred twenty people to the venue in two hours. Maybe for thirty people," the frantic caterer had said.

"Great," Simone had replied. "Bring the food as soon as possible." She had called three other gourmet eateries and ordered food for thirty people from each location. The happy couple had been pleased to see Greek food as well as Italian, Indian, and Turkish. They gave Simone and Jennifer a very generous bonus for saving their day. If it weren't for them, the wedding could have been a disaster.

Simone turned to Jennifer, "You and I need to strategize and brainstorm before meeting with the police. If you're thinking what I'm thinking, we might have more than just a dead bride on our hands. We might be planning a funeral."

CHAPTER 24

Two Greenwich Police Officers, and a Grand Hamilton Hotel security officer met Jennifer, Simone, Charlie, and Frederick in Conference Room 106. They sat around an oval mahogany table, except for Frederick who stood with his back against the wall near the door.

"Good afternoon. I'm Officer John McGuire with the Greenwich Police Department. I'm the lead investigating officer for this case. Officer Michael Powers will be taking notes." After brief introductions, Officer McGuire said, "Miss Keys, please tell us what you witnessed in Miss Bouvier's room."

Nervously, Jennifer began, "After Simone and I checked the banquet hall, I went to Mrs. Bouvier's room. The maid-of-honor was there too. They were visibly upset over Casey's wellbeing. I assumed the ladies also saw Casey's erratic behavior, the same that Simone and I had seen."

Jennifer took a drink of water, and continued, "I told the women that Casey was a nervous bride; we've seen this before. We actually don't see brides acting this extreme," Jennifer added, "but I wanted to console them. I assured them I would calm Casey down, and they should return to her room at 3:00, in time for photographs. Then, I went to Casey's room."

"What time was that?" the officer asked.

"Around 1:30."

"Did she answer the door?"

"No. I knocked, but no answer."

"How did you get in?"

"Simone and I are always given a key to the bride's room in case the bride forgets something before the ceremony. During the reception, one of us returns to the bride's room and works with housekeeping to clean and prepare it for the wedding night."

"Please, just tell us what happened after you arrived at the bride's room," said the officer impatiently.

"I went into Casey's room and found her fully dressed. Her hair and makeup were done. She was all alone, sitting at her dressing table staring straight ahead, not moving. I went up to her and asked, 'Casey, are you alright?' She didn't answer. I called out for Hilda, but she wasn't around."

"Who's Hilda?" the officer asked.

"She's the hair and makeup stylist." Jennifer turned to Simone, "She did a great job by the way, in such a short amount of time. . ."

"Please, continue telling us what happened," Officer McGuire cut her off again. "Was there anyone else in, or near the room?"

"No, no one else. I did notice the fire exit door closing as I was knocking on Casey's door, but I didn't see anyone, so I ignored it."

"What happened next?" McGuire asked.

Jennifer continued, "I waved my hand in front of Casey's face and she didn't blink. I remember seeing a little trickle of blood dripping from her nose; it stained her dress. I poked her arm, and that's when she fell to the floor. I felt for a pulse and she didn't have one. I grabbed the hotel phone, and told the operator to send a doctor. I started CPR. The doctor took over when he arrived. That's all I remember."

Officer McGuire asked, "So you told Mrs. Bouvier that her daughter was high on drugs?"

"No. I didn't say that," Jennifer snapped. "I told her it wasn't unusual for a bride to be nervous on her wedding day."

"Then you forced your way into Miss Bouvier's room."

"Are you not listening?" Jennifer said impatiently, her voice elevating. "I did not force my way into Casey's room. I had a key."

"She works with me," Simone interjected hoping to stop the badgering. "We've been in business together for several years. I'll give you a statement as well."

The hotel officer, Robert Hathaway, sat across from Simone, with his back to the door and to Frederick. He asked, "Miss Simpson, can you tell me where you were and what you were doing before you got the call about Miss Bouvier?"

"I can tell you where she was, and what she was doing," interrupted Frederick playing house detective.

Simone could sense Charlie's body tightening, as well as her own. She might only be 5'1", but she had a temper that could rival any one, no matter their size. She had had it with Frederick. She pushed her chair back with such force that it rolled back and hit the wall behind her. She walked over to Frederick and stood in front of him.

"Is he talking to you?" With her voice raised, she continued, "And what can you tell this officer I was doing? Were you in the room? Did you hear my conversation?"

"No ma'am," Frederick said, embarrassed.

"Miss Simpson," she heard Officer McGuire say. "Please sit down."

"Simone," Jennifer said. She was shocked at Simone's lack of discipline. She admired her boss' ability to stay calm. This action was very unusual.

"Don't ever answer for me again," Simone continued.

"Yes, ma'am."

"Miss Simpson, sit down," commanded Officer McGuire, louder.

Charlie rose from his chair. He walked over to Simone, put his hands on her elbow and pulled her away from Frederick. He escorted her back to the table, as he moved her chair back into place. She had lost control, which was uncharacteristic, but she wasn't going to allow anyone to accuse her, or Jennifer, of any inappropriate actions.

"So Miss Simpson," Officer Hathaway continued.

"Excuse me, Officer Hathaway," Officer McGuire interrupted. "I believe this is the town's investigation. We'd appreciate you leaving the inquiry to us."

The tension in the room between the town officer and the hotel officer was palpable.

McGuire continued, "Miss Simpson, please tell us all where you where, and what you were doing while all this was happening with Miss Bouvier."

"I was in Mr. Hamilton's office discussing Miss Bouvier's behavior." She quickly glanced at Frederick, who kept his eyes averted. "We suspected she was high on drugs. We found bottles of Xanax and Valium in her bathroom, along with a glass of wine, and empty wine bottles in the trash bin. I asked Mr. Hamilton if I could call the hotel doctor, and ask him to be in attendance at the ceremony."

"So, you weren't in the room when Miss Bouvier died?" he asked.

Simone kept her temper under control. "No sir, I wasn't in the room. As I said, I was in Mr. Hamilton's office at the time."

A thought came to her. "But, I believe Frederick was in the room. Come to think of it, I don't know why Frederick didn't call Mr. Hamilton's office from the bridal suite, instead of leaving Jennifer there doing CPR." *Don't ever try to throw me under the bus,* Simone thought.

Officer McGuire turned to Frederick. The blood drained from his face. He grabbed an empty chair and sat down, his blue eyes glared at Simone.

"Frederick, did you see Miss Bouvier before Jennifer got there?" McGuire asked.

"No sir," he answered a bit too loudly. "I heard the call for EMS on my walkie, so I ran upstairs to see if I could help."

Again, his walkie didn't sit well with Simone.

"And what did you see when you got there?"

"I saw Miss Keys administering CPR on Miss Bouvier. Well, I think it was CPR. She was kneeling next to her, with her back to the door pounding down on her chest."

Charlie grabbed Simone's hand. They locked eyes. He slowly shook his head as if to say, leave it alone. He sensed Simone was going to morph into a Pit bull and latch her jaws into Frederick.

"Frederick, do you know how to administer CPR?" McGuire asked him.

"No sir, I've never been trained."

"So what makes you think she wasn't administering CPR?"

"It just looked so violent."

Ignoring McGuire's instructions and cutting him off mid-sentence, Officer Hathaway looked at Jennifer and asked, "Are you trained in CPR?"

"Yes, both Simone and I are trained. It was a requirement when I joined Simone's team. She wants all of her associates trained in CPR, first aid, self-defense, and to observe our clients for any kind of drug or alcohol abuse."

"And why is that?" McGuire took control again, while giving Officer Hathaway a stern look.

"Because we've seen lots of people anxious over their big day, and quite often they turn to drugs or alcohol to calm their nerves. Sometimes, brides who had been fasting, detoxing, or juicing just to lose those extra pounds before the wedding, consume drugs or alcohol. And it can have a devastating effect."

"Thank you," Officer Hathaway said, again, ignoring McGuire. He stared at Jennifer a little bit longer than necessary.

"You're welcome," she acknowledged, while doing a quick glance for signs of a ring on his left hand.

Although Hathaway also carried a gun, Simone bet he was nothing more than a Rent-A-Cop who worked on the Hamilton property. Cop or no cop, she didn't trust him.

Simone thought him to be around thirty. He was overweight, had a shaved head, and the top of a tattoo was visible from his shirt collar.

Jennifer gave him a seductive look, which he returned with a sly grin.

Not a good time, Jennifer, Simone thought.

Officer McGuire asked everyone to hand over their driver's licenses to Officer Powers, and to also provide their contact information.

After taking statements from the two sets of parents, the bridal party and Patrick, Officer Jones arrived in the conference room. He helped Officer Powers obtain the remaining pertinent information.

Hathaway gave Jennifer his direct cell number in case she had any questions, or remembered something important relating to the case. In return he asked to receive a copy of her driver's license and contact information.

Simone was concerned about Jennifer taking a liking to Hathaway. In the past she had been attracted to "bad boys" and he fit that description. Except, this bad boy carried a gun.

CHAPTER 25

At 4:00 pm, Conference Room 106 was filled with Casey's weary-eyed parents, her brother, Patrick and his parents, Charlie, Frederick, Simone and Jennifer.

"Mr. and Mrs. Bouvier, once again, I can't tell you how sorry we are for your loss," Simone said sympathetically.

Simone addressed Patrick, who sat with his head down. "I can't imagine what you're going through as well." His response: a sniffle.

"What's this all about," a very impatient Mr. Bouvier demanded. "The cops told us we can't leave the hotel until they finish doing an initial investigation and get statements from all of us. I've never heard of such a thing. We'll see what our attorney, Jeremy, has to say about this. I told him he . . ."

"Bruce, please," said Mrs. Bouvier cutting him off. "Enough. Let's hear what Simone wants so we can go back to our rooms." This was the first time Simone saw Mrs. Bouvier stand up to her husband.

"Mr. and Mrs. Bouvier," interjected Charlie. "Again, please know that we at the Grand Hamilton Hotel extend our deepest sympathies."

"Thank you," said Mrs. Bouvier. Mr. Bouvier mumbled something unintelligible.

Simone stood up, and walked over, handing them a piece of paper. "What's this? Your bill?"

"Bruce, stop it. Please."

"Sorry," he said with less agitation.

Simone gave a copy to Charlie, Frederick, and her staff. She sat back down and waited for reality to sink in, and for the arguing to start.

Mr. and Mrs. Bouvier and family,

Mr. and Mrs. Michaelson, Patrick, and family,

Jennifer, Katy, Jonathan, and I are deeply saddened by Casey's passing.

We ask that you allow us to continue to work with you this evening, and to diffuse some of your burden. Your guests will be arriving shortly, learn about Casey's passing and that the wedding has been cancelled; some will return home. Their shock and dismay will add to your grief.

They will want to talk to you, and ask you what happened. Unless you're willing to be prisoners in your rooms, you'll have to face your guests. Or, if the police give you permission, leave the hotel as soon as possible before any guests arrive

Your guests would have spent a considerable amount of money on a ho-tel room, transportation, airfare, car rentals, clothes, etc. Your financial loss, over $400,000, is much more considerable. You've already paid for the wedding gown, the flowers, hotel, your attire, etc. You will still need to pay for the banquet hall, the musicians, photographer, flowers, wed-ding planning services, and all the other vendors involved. You might recover some of the money through your wedding insurance policy, but not a significant amount.

Jennifer and I would like to recommend having Casey's memorial this evening.

"Are you out of your mind?" shouted Mr. Bouvier.

Simone quickly added, "I know this might sound insensitive, but hear me out, before you say anything."

"Simone," Charlie whispered. "What are you doing?" He sounded shocked by her callousness.

"Trust me, Charlie," she whispered back. He shook his head in disbelief.

"Insensitive, hard-hearted . . . you're crazy," Mr. Bouvier yelled.

"Let me explain," begged Simone, interrupting his rhetoric. She stood up. Feeling a combination of anxiety, fear and determination, she continued. "In about two hours you will have over three hundred people arriving for your daughter's wedding. They have traveled from distant destinations. Everyone who loves Casey will be here in attendance.

"Jennifer, our staff and I will work with the hotel in creating a more reserved setting. We will ask Father John, who was doing the marriage ceremony, to lead the memorial service. We will still use the ceremony hall for the service, then your guests can go to the banquet hall to eat the food you've already paid for.

"No assigned seating. My staff has already rearranged the flowers and tables, released the photographer and the band members. Any indication of wedding festivities will be omitted. The brightly colored tablecloths will be replaced with dark colored cloths."

She continued, "We won't have a cocktail hour, a carving station, pasta station, or Venetian hour. All the food will be served buffet, allowing us to take food allocated for the cocktail hour to be incorporated into the dinner. The bar will be minimal. We will remove the wedding cake, and serve cookies instead.

"You can stay as long as you like at the memorial. Your friends and family will certainly understand if you leave before the end of the reception.

"It is an excellent use of everyone's time, and prevents you from a large financial impact. I'm not putting a price tag on Casey, trust me, I'm not. But you're already losing a lot of money, regardless if this takes place or not. If you have a memorial in the future, the same people will have to travel again and you will have an added expense, as will your guests. This might sound cold-hearted, but you've got a captive audience, and you should take advantage of the situation."

Simone pointed to her assistants. "Since Jennifer and I have to remove ourselves from this, Katy and Jonathan are more than qualified to step in. Also, since Mr. Hamilton will not be here going forward, another banquet manager will be the point person. We are waiting for an answer from the police if Frederick can stay involved. Jennifer, Mr. Hamilton and I will be available by phone or text if anything arises, or if you have any questions. Everyone is just waiting for your approval."

Simone sat down and waited for the Bouviers' anger to rise, and the screaming to begin. She felt surprisingly strong. Given the circumstances, she knew in her heart and from her experience, the plan she and Jennifer put forth was the ideal solution for this family.

No one said a word. There was absolute silence, except for Charlie clicking his pen, as he read over the paper in front of him.

She was either going to be perceived as a genius, or a cold-hearted lunatic. Simone broke the silence and rose from her chair. "I think at this time, my personal staff, and the hotel staff, should step out of the room, and allow the families to discuss their options."

"No," boomed Mr. Bouvier. Simone jumped at his voice. He stood up and walked towards her. She braced herself for his reaction.

"No, no need to leave the room," he said in a gentler voice. "Simone, you're brilliant. I would have never thought this through as thoroughly as you have."

He turned to his wife. "Mother, what do you say? We honor our baby girl on her special day? If our guests think this is crazy, they can go home, and attend her funeral. I think it's a very good idea."

Mrs. Bouvier began to cry. Then, she collected herself and wiped her eyes. "I don't know. All of this is such a shock. I suppose it's a good idea, if just a bit unconventional." Her fingers slid to rubbing her pearls. "What will our relatives think? What will our friends say? What will be the Fitzgeralds' reaction? Oh, my, Bruce, the Fitzgeralds. I don't think I can face them." She turned to the groom, "Patrick, what do you think?"

He responded with a sniffle.

Patrick's parents sat nearby not saying a word. After all, it was the Bouviers who were paying for the wedding. They didn't have much to contribute to the decision. They didn't know if their relatives would stay for a memorial, or not. Mrs. Michaelson put her hand on Patrick's, but he pulled away.

Simone looked at Charlie, trying to get a handle on what he was thinking. She thought she detected tears in his eyes. "You okay?" she whispered.

He looked up at her, "Yes. You're amazing," he responded.

Simone took charge again, "Frederick, please work with Katy and Jonathan. Inform everyone what needs to be done, and then, if ordered by the police, you can remove yourself from the event." She handed him a small stack of papers. "Meanwhile, here are some thoughts we put together on rearranging the banquet hall and the ceremony room.

"While guests arrive for the ceremony, the family can be off in another room. Once everyone is seated, Mr. Bouvier, or Father John, can make a statement about the day's events. Katy can help you write up a brief statement asking everyone to respect your wishes, and to ask questions after the memorial ceremony. We will tweak the details as we get closer to 6:00."

She turned to her assistants, "Katy and Jonathan, I'll be available for you at a moment's notice. Mr. and Mrs. Bouvier, I hope you understand that Jennifer and I can't help at this point, especially since Jennifer was so personally involved. If you all are in agreement, we need to move very quickly to get things set up."

"We understand," they said in unison.

Everyone stood up and started to leave.

"Thank you, Simone and Jennifer," said Mrs. Bouvier. She walked over to them and gave them each a hug, followed with hugs by Mr. Bouvier.

Mr. and Mrs. Michaelson also came over to the planners, and shook their hands. "Thank you so much, Miss Simpson," said Mr. Michaelson. "You're doing a fantastic job helping us deal with enormous shock."

Mrs. Michaelson walked over to Mrs. Bouvier. The two women looked at each other, and both began to cry for the loss of a daughter, a future daughter-in-law, and for the horror of the whole event.

It was agreed that the two families would meet Frederick, the substitute banquet manager, and Katy back in the ceremony room at 5:45. They would keep the doors to the room locked, so no guests would be allowed in until precisely 6:00. Jonathan would do his best to keep inquiring guests, who may have already heard the news, from spreading unfounded rumors. It would be difficult, but it could be done.

"I'll be right back," Jennifer said to Simone. She left the conference room, Simone assuming, to use the ladies' room.

The Bouviers' headed back to their rooms to gather their thoughts, and to change clothes. Simone assumed that Patrick was going back to his room to get high. Charlie went back to his office to make the dreaded call to his father, asking for a substitute banquet manager, and inform him how the wedding would now be changed to a memorial, honoring the late bride. "Unconventional" was an understatement.

When Simone left the conference room she saw Jennifer talking to rent-a-cop, Bob Hathaway. She overheard him saying, "I'd love to have dinner with you tonight. We could go into town. I know this great burger joint that has a jazz band on Saturday nights."

"I don't think I can. I need to stay here, in case they need me. I'll probably have dinner with Simone."

"Hey Jennifer," Simone interrupted. She heard enough of their conversation to make her stomach turn. It was bad enough that she had to cross the line and suggest transferring a wedding into a memorial, but now Hathaway wanted to go out and party.

"Office Hathaway, I need to talk to Jennifer. Excuse us."

She took Jennifer by the arm and moved her away from earshot of Hathaway. "Jennifer, we've known each other a very long time. I've never told you what to do, but now, I'm recommending that you be very careful. You're part of an investigation, it's not proper to spend time with an investigating officer."

Jennifer stared at Simone, feeling as if she was being reprimanded for talking to Bob Hathaway. This was the first time Simone ever intruded in her personal life, but maybe she had a point.

"He seems pleasant enough and didn't try to twist my words around like the other cop. I don't think you need to be concerned," Jennifer answered, seemingly annoyed.

Simone was taken aback, but chalked it up to post traumatic stress. After all, she did try to revive a dead person today.

"Jennifer, we both need to stay around the hotel and be available for any further questioning by the police. Why don't you go back to your room and relax. I'll call you if you're needed. You've been through a lot today. I'll keep in touch with Katy and Jonathan on the details. Charlie is requesting additional staff, so it should all be done very quickly. I admire the way you handled yourself. I'm very lucky to have you by my side," Simone said sincerely. "I'm going to the bar, to observe from the sidelines what's going on, and be available if Katy or Jonathan have any questions. I want to be sure everything is running smoothly. After the conclusion of the memorial service, while the guests are in the banquet hall, we can go to the Tavern for a relaxing dinner. I'll make a reservation for 7:45. We'll charge dinner to the groom's room," Simone said, trying to interject a light note.

"Simone, I appreciate you looking out for me. But I'm a big girl and can take care of myself."

"I know you are. But you've also been through a very traumatic experience. I'm just worried about you."

"Thanks, Simone. No worries. I'll tell Bob that I'm having dinner with you. I'll see you later." With that, Jennifer turned away and walked back to Officer Bob Hathaway.

Simone watched them walk off in the direction of the café. She turned, sauntered past the bar, and looked around the lobby to see if Frederick was lurking behind a post. She stopped at the sundries counter, her purchase placed in a brown bag, and then headed straight to Charlie's office.

She knocked.

"Come in."

Simone entered. Charlie, his head down, was writing. A baseball game was on the TV. He paused and looked up. "Hey Simone," he said with a big smile.

"Hey Charlie." She closed the door behind her. She quickly glanced at the TV. "Want to play a quick game of "baseball" before I have to go back to work?" she whispered in a seductive voice. "Interested in some 'condom"ments?'" She tossed the brown bag to him.

"Simone, I like the way you play," he chuckled.

She locked the door and pulled the office chair, wedging it under the door handle. A disturbing memory flashed through her mind, when, years ago, another chair once kept out a different monster – her father. This time, the monster was Frederick.

She switched off the light. The only illumination was from the flickering of the TV.

Charlie stood up and watched Simone slowly remove her messenger bag from across her chest. She unbuttoned her white shirt, and tossed it on the chair behind her. She flipped off her shoes and removed her slacks. She stood in front of Charlie wearing a white lace thong and matching bra, showing off her trim, firm body.

Charlie pushed the papers off his desk and onto the floor. He stripped off his clothes, letting them randomly fall around him.

Simone slowly approached Charlie's desk. He tore at her bra and panties, as he passionately kissed her mouth. Her body responded with intense hunger and yearning, her desire for him being completely satisfied.

CHAPTER 26

Simone and Jennifer sat at a table on the patio at the Tavern Restaurant. It was 8:00, with another hour or so of daylight left. They were being rewarded with a beautiful sunset and a cool breeze off Long Island Sound. The memorial service had gone on as planned, and now the guests were in the banquet hall. It went well, despite the pervasive melancholy mood.

As she studied the menu, Jennifer said, "This is a big change from just a couple of hours ago." She looked towards the sun, closed her eyes and drank in the warmth. She seemed more relaxed, the tension between them gone. She softly said, "I'm sorry things got a little weird before. I think the stress just got to me."

Simone wondered if when they parted ways after the planning meeting, had Jennifer taken Bob Hathaway back to her room. "No problem, Jennifer. Just as long as we continue to talk to each other. I don't want anything to come between us. We've been friends and business partners for a long time. I'd like it to continue that way."

Jennifer gave her a big smile, and studied the menu.

Simone was feeling exhausted. It was a day of roller coaster emotions beginning with the normal stresses of a wedding day, followed by Casey's death, the quickie with Charlie, and her annoyance at Jennifer for her attraction towards Rent-A-Cop. There was something about him that made Simone's skin crawl.

As they listened to the waiter drone on about the fresh catch of the day, Simone heard a voice behind her, "Hello ladies." Jennifer's face began to flush. "May I join you?" It was Bob Hathaway. Suddenly, Simone realized who he reminded her of: Nagini, the snake in the Harry Potter book. His beady brown eyes and bald head enhanced the resemblance.

"Sure," Simone answered before Jennifer could respond. She just smiled at her partner and mouthed, "We're cool." Simone realized she was feeling a little guilty for chastising Jennifer about him. She wasn't thrilled at the thought of spending time with him, but maybe her suspicions would be quelled.

He was dressed in jeans and a white Oxford shirt, which enhanced his tan. His sleeves were rolled up displaying his muscular forearms painted with numerous, colorful tattoos.

"May I buy you ladies a drink? Waiter, a bottle of prosecco please with three glasses," he ordered. When Hathaway raised his arm, his shirt sleeve moved upward, exposing a tattoo of a snake, entwined around a strand of Rosary beads, and the initials, CAB.

Simone was immediately transported back to the cold, rainy night in December years ago, when her husband, Joe, was killed by a cab and died in her arms. She wondered if Hathaway had similarly lost someone he loved.

Simone snapped back to the sound of Charlie's voice, "Make that four glasses." The announcement came from behind her. "May I join you, too?"

"Sure," Jennifer said brightly before Simone could respond.

"Touché, Jennifer," Simone whispered to her partner, followed by a smile.

Charlie had changed out of his uniform, into jeans and a light blue polo shirt. Simone had only seen him in his uniform, or naked. This was a departure and a nice treat for her.

Charlie kept himself in good shape, positive results from using the hotel's gym.

As they scanned the menu, Simone kept humming a song that was stuck in her head.

Charlie leaned towards her and asked, "What's that you're humming?"

"Paradise by the Dashboard Light by Meat Loaf. You know it? Phil Rizzuto has a big part."

Charlie emitted a loud laugh. And, with a big grin on his face he said, "I remember that song very well, and now I will remember it forever."

CHAPTER 27

After dinner, the two couples moved to the bar and listened to the piano player croon love songs. Guests at the memorial had left, the two families back in their rooms. Simone thought about Mrs. Bouvier, and how she must be feeling. Poor woman, Simone thought, her eyes filmed. She couldn't imagine what it would be like to lose a child. Wait, she did.

"What'll be?" asked the bartender, bringing her out of her thoughts.

"I'll have a club soda with cranberry juice," Simone answered.

Her head was buzzed from the two bottles of prosecco they had shared with dinner, and she needed to stay alert. Charlie ordered a single malt scotch. Jennifer followed Simone's lead, and Bob ordered a beer.

"Simone," Charlie whispered, putting one hand on her thigh and sliding the other one along the mahogany bar. A bolt of electricity ran through her. "You know, I'm falling in love with you."

"Charlie, it's the booze talking," she whispered back, as she removed his hand from her leg. "One passionate quickie on top of your desk and you're going soft on me," she said semi-joking.

"It's not the booze, Simone, and you know it. And I'm far from being soft," he said with a teasing twinkle in his eyes.

"Can we talk about this another time? I really don't want to give Jennifer, Hathaway, or anyone else in this hotel the wrong impression of our working relationship," using air quotes with her fingers for "working."

He continued, "Please spend the night with me."

"Are you out of your mind, Charlie?" she said a bit too loudly. She quickly clapped her hand over her mouth once she realized how loudly she said the words.

Jennifer, who was sitting behind Charlie, swiveled her chair around and asked, "Is everything okay?"

Trying to change the subject, Simone responded, "Yes, Charlie just offered us a job as in-house wedding planners. I told him, unless he's willing to pay us each $250,000, he'll have to find another set of gals."

"So, Charlie, what do you say? Aren't we worth it?" Jennifer said with a smirk. "Simone is selling us short at that price."

Frederick suddenly showed up. "Mr. Hamilton, may I speak with you for a few minutes? The Bouviers want to go over the final details of the memorial."

Hathaway swung around, his back to Frederick, and ordered another beer.

"Now, at this hour? It's 11:15. Tell them I'll be happy to go over the details with them in the morning."

Frederick looked slowly at Jennifer, Charlie and then Simone, extending his look a few extra beats at Simone. The music escalated, keeping in tempo with Frederick's stares. She wondered how much he saw before he told Charlie that the Bouviers wanted to talk to him. Did he see Charlie whispering in her ear with his hand on her thigh? Did the Bouviers really want to talk to him now, or was Frederick using that as a ploy to get him away from her? Frederick turned away, and walked out.

"So tell me Charlie," Simone said. "Who is that guy? Why does he always seem to butt into other people's conversations, and show up at inappropriate moments? It looks as if he has it in for you."

"He's Frederick H. Murphy," he answered, with an emphasis on the H. "He's been working here on and off every summer for about ten years. He's a computer geek. He programs our computers, phone system, does maintenance. He's also worked as a server and sometimes, as a caddy. This past month he was promoted to assistant banquet manager. The promotion has gone to his head."

"What's the "H" stand for?" As Simone asked the question, she got a sick feeling in her stomach.

Charlie hesitated before responding. He looked into Simone's eyes and answered, "Hamilton."

"Ah, Hamilton." Simone said. "In a way, I'm not surprised. It all makes sense now."

"He's one of my sister, Harriet's boys. One of her four. He expects to assume my job, move me out, and take over the Hamilton estate. The way things are going, it won't be too long before that happens. I have a feeling that he reports back to my father about me . . . all my actions, mistakes, hotel problems, indiscretions." Charlie chuckled at this last word. "Frederick graduated from Princeton with a degree in technology, and thinks he's a know-it-all."

"Oh Charlie, I had no idea."

Did he say Princeton? Simone pondered.

Before Charlie got emotional, she announced, "We'd better break up this party." She looked at her watch. It was 11:30. "We all have a full day ahead of us. By the way, Bob, were the police able to talk to Hilda, the stylist?"

"I haven't heard anything yet. Earlier this evening, we sent our officers to her apartment in Rye." Simone instinctively felt he was lying, and that he had nothing to do with sending 'our officers' to her apartment. Even though Simone tried to get to know Bob during dinner, there was something about him that caused her suspicions to be roused. She still didn't like, or trust him.

"Well, if you don't need Jennifer and me any longer, we have to get some sleep. We'll be leaving early in the morning. We need to get back to Fairfield to pack for our trip to Los Angeles."

"Oh, didn't I tell you?" Jennifer said. "We got a call from LA. The wedding is off."

Simone looked shocked. Was Jennifer playing some sort of 'let's get even' game, punishing her for suggesting she not have dinner with Hathaway? This was very uncharacteristic of her. They were business partners and relied on each other for updates.

"When did they call, and when did you plan to tell me?" Simone asked, with a firm, annoyed voice. "Were you going to wait until I drove to the airport tomorrow?"

"They called around 5:00, our time," Jennifer answered.

"And you're telling me now?" Simone's annoyance was rising, and Jennifer realized she had crossed the line. It was rare that Simone got angry with Jennifer, but this time, Jennifer was wrong, and she knew it.

"I'm sorry. I guess I forgot to mention it. I came looking for you at the bar, but I couldn't find you." Jennifer snuck a quick glance at Charlie and back to Simone. Simone didn't respond, doing her best to keep a poker face. Jennifer suspected something was going on between her and Charlie, and had thought so for some time. The less questions Simone and Jennifer asked each other about their personal lives, the better.

As in the past, their unspoken words were communication enough.

Jennifer got off the bar stool and walked up to Simone, so that only Simone could hear what she was saying. The piano player ramped up his volume as the bar became more crowded. "Simone, I'm sorry. I forgot to tell you."

Simone mumbled, "It's okay."

Jennifer continued, "Since we don't have to leave early in the morning, I'd like to go to Bob's for an after dinner drink. You don't mind, do you?" asking the question as though she were addressing a parent. Simone ignored the inflection. Jennifer glanced again at Charlie and back at Simone, "I'll be back in the morning around 9:00."

"Jen, if I were you, I wouldn't make any assumptions," Simone said, firmly. In all the years working together, they sometimes disagreed, but they had never had a fight. Now, Simone felt Jennifer was crossing a line, but she attributed it to the stresses of the day and moved on.

Simone was embarrassed and angry at herself for giving away any hint of her relationship with Charlie. She kept her dating life private, and never wanted an employee to have too much information about her personal life that could possibly be used at some point in the future.

"My friend here had a lot to drink. But thanks for letting me know when you'll be back. I don't want to send out a search party at 3:00 in the morning," Simone said flatly.

"If you'd like, I can text you when I get back to the hotel, Jennifer said with a snarky tone.

"That's not necessary, Jennifer. Just be ready to leave by checkout."

Simone did not agree with Jennifer's loose lifestyle. But Simone wasn't her mother. This wasn't the first time Jennifer had hooked up with a guy she met at a bar, or at a party.

"I'm going to bed. I'll see you all in the morning," Simone announced. She looked at her lover. "Good night, Charlie. I'll see you tomorrow before we check out."

She left him at the bar nursing his scotch.

CHAPTER 28

Simone returned to her room. The day's stress hit her; she was exhausted, her mind in a brain fog. She wanted a shower and she needed a good night's sleep.

She had just gotten out of the shower, when she heard a knock at the door. She grabbed the hotel bathrobe and wrapped herself in its luxury. She looked through the peephole but saw no one. She walked into the bathroom, turned on the water, and brushed her teeth. The knock returned, but this time, it was coming from the connecting door.

She stood in front of it and stared. Another knock. Without a doubt she knew who was going to be on the other side. She unlatched the brass lock, opened the door, and came face to face with Charlie.

"This is why I got this room – it connects to your new living quarters."

"Find any dead brides under your bed, my dear?" Charlie said while wringing his hands, his back slightly hunched over like the Big Bad Wolf. "May I come in and look?"

For some inexplicable reason, Simone found this statement hysterical. The day's drama took over her good senses.

Although she was exhausted, she was also aroused. The shower brought her renewed energy. *What was it about him that makes me lose all control?* Simone wondered.

She slowly untied the thick white belt of her robe. She wanted him, desperately, in so many ways: to make the day's horrors go away, to make her feel safe, to make her feel like a vibrant woman. She dropped the robe enough to expose her bare shoulders. An audible gasp came from Charlie. He moved towards her, gently placed his hands on her soft bare skin and pushed the rest of the robe off her body.

"You're beautiful," he murmured and began kissing her passionately. Charlie picked her up and carried her to the bed, while drinking in her nakedness. He peeled off his clothes in seconds flat. "Should I check for the boogie man first?"

"I think he's straddling me," she quipped.

CHAPTER 29

At 1:00 am Simone called room service. "A double order of fries, a bottle of prosecco, and a glass of single malt scotch. Room 1017. Only one person. Thank you."

While they waited for the food, Charlie and Simone sat on the sofa, each wrapped in hotel bathrobes. They discussed the possible cause of Casey's death. The conversation went from serious, to speculation, to "she deserved it."

"Do you really think it was an overdose, or did someone knock her off?" Charlie asked. "You've been working with her for about a year, did she have any enemies?"

"She is a . . . was a . . . bridezilla. She was demanding, nasty, and felt entitled. When I first met her, she was a ponytail-bopping young woman, who, over time, changed . . . more insufferable. I'm sure there's a plethora of people who wanted her dead."

There was a knock at the door. Charlie hurried back to his room closing the connecting door behind him. Simone secured her bathrobe, and took a quick look around. Charlie's clothes were in a pile on the floor near the bed. "Just a moment," she shouted, as she quickly pushed the clothes out of sight.

When she looked through the peephole, she saw the fish-eyed face of Frederick.

She opened the door. "What do you want?" she snapped.

"I brought your food."

"How did you know . . . never mind. Just put it over there," she pointed to the table in the sitting area. She was too tired to try to figure it out. She was starting to wonder if Frederick had planted a secret bug inside her room.

As she signed the check, Frederick took a look around the room. He noticed the unmade bed, and the safety latch on the connecting door was not engaged. He knew the scotch was for Charlie, and that his uncle's room was on the other side of that connecting door.

Simone watched him take in the surroundings. When Frederick locked his eyes on the connecting door she interrupted his thoughts, "Lose something?"

"No," he stammered. "Good night, Ms. Simpson." He left the room, closing the door behind him.

She shut off the lights in the room and opened the connecting door. There was Charlie, a silhouette against his room's lamplight, completely naked, with a necktie on his fully erect penis. She gave him an approving look from head to toe. His boyish grin made him look like a teenager.

She emitted a giggle, grabbed the necktie in her hand, and pulled him close to her. "Maybe she hung herself." That got both of them giggling.

He slowly removed Simone's robe and started kissing her neck and then her breasts. She arched her back, her head facing the hotel room door.

There was a dark shadow moving under the door, as if someone was standing nearby.

She gently pushed Charlie away and placed her finger to her lips and whispered, "Shh. Hold that thought."

She lifted the cloche, quickly grabbed a handful of hot French fries, devoured them with gusto, and cautiously, walked toward the door.

Charlie went back into his room, again shutting the door between them. Simone secured her robe. She looked through the peep hole and saw Frederick's profile against the door. Furtively, she flung open the door. Frederick nearly fell on top of her. "Still looking for something, Frederick?"

His face turned red. He muttered that he had dropped something.

"Funny, I saw your head against my door when I looked through the peephole. Did I not tip you enough? Got a problem, Frederick, or do I need to call security?" she commanded.

He turned away from her, and he sprinted to the exit door. She yelled after him, her voice echoing throughout the empty hallway, possibly disturbing sleeping guests. "If I ever find you lurking at my door again I'll have you arrested."

She put the Do Not Disturb sign on the knob, and bolted the door with the security latch. She dragged a chair from the desk, and wedged it under the doorknob. Again, she flashbacked to the midnight monster; they come in all shapes and sizes.

She welcomed Charlie back to her bed. Afterwards they shared the remaining cold, greasy fries and the bottle of prosecco.

In the morning, Simone stood in the oversized shower and let the jets pulsate soothing water over her body. She tried to wash away her confused feelings towards Charlie. His face danced in her mind as she relived the incredible lovemaking of the night before. She greatly desired Charlie, but could never love him.

Or could she?

That thought lingered long after the day was over.

CHAPTER 30

There was a knock on Charlie's office door. Before he could say anything, it opened, and in walked Frederick, followed by the Bouviers.

Charlie stood up slowly, "Good morning Mr. and Mrs. Bouvier. Please sit down. Can I get you anything – coffee, tea?"

"No, thank you. We just finished breakfast with some of our guests."

Charlie nodded at Frederick as to say, 'Get lost.'

Frederick closed the door behind him, but Charlie was certain his ear was pressed up against the door, eavesdropping on their conversation.

"I trust, given the circumstances of yesterday's event, you felt support from family and friends. Again, my deepest sympathies to you both on your daughter's passing. I think you and your family made the best of the situation having Miss Bouvier's memorial."

"Well, we had time to think, and we're not so sure now. It was such a great shock to all of us," said Mrs. Bouvier as she began to cry. "Honestly, my husband and I now think we were pushed into doing Casey's memorial by Simone."

Charlie's head was pounding. In retrospect, perhaps he and Simone should not have ordered the bottle of prosecco and scotch. The cold, undigested fries felt like a lump in his stomach.

He continued, "When we left the conference room yesterday you thought it was a brilliant idea to have the memorial. What's happened since then? As Ms. Simpson pointed out, you would have lost hundreds of thousands of dollars if you canceled the event."

Charlie opened his desk drawer, grabbed a bottle of Advil and washed down three pills with his leftover coffee. He continued, "Frederick reported the memorial went very well."

Mrs. Bouvier started, "We had to explain the situation to hundreds of people. A lot of them thought it was disrespectful to have the memorial last night."

"Now, now Mother. Most of the people thought it was a very good idea," said Mr. Bouvier. "They appreciated not having to pay a lot of money to get here, and then having it canceled. You're just upset over what Jeremy told us."

"Who is Jeremy?" Charlie asked.

"Our attorney. He said that if Casey died as a result of negligence, due in part because of the hotel, we can file a lawsuit. He thinks maybe the hotel was covering something up, that's why you pushed to do the memorial. Also, he's questioning the validity of the wedding insurance. Doesn't that cover our daughter's death?"

Charlie couldn't believe what he was hearing. Late yesterday afternoon, they couldn't have been more supportive of the idea, thinking Simone was a genius. They had thanked them both profusely for transitioning the banquet hall into a more respectful setting.

"I'd suggest, Mr. Bouvier, that you have your attorney review all the contracts: the one with the Grand Hamilton Hotel, all the vendors, and the wedding insurance contract."

Switching subjects, Mrs. Bouvier said, "You don't look very well, Mr. Hamilton."

"I beg your pardon?"

"Did you spend the whole night with Simone and Jennifer partying at my daughter's expense?"

Quickly Mr. Bouvier interrupted, "Amanda." The pet name of 'Mother' was dropped. "We don't know if all of that is true."

"What are you talking about, Mrs. Bouvier?" Charlie's rage was starting to creep up. He could feel his cheeks getting warm. He had a major hangover and was functioning on little sleep. Dealing with these two was the last thing he wanted to contend with this morning. "You don't know if what is true?" Charlie tried to keep his voice steady and his evolving temper under control. He started to rise out of his chair, but his pounding head forced him to sit down again.

"Well, we heard from a reliable source that you spent the night drinking and partying with Simone and Jennifer, while we were downstairs mourning our daughter's passing."

"Mr. and Mrs. Bouvier that is a very offensive accusation. I have no idea who told you such a thing." But he had a good idea who did. Charlie held his tongue. "Be assured, I was not celebrating your daughter's passing. As you know, by order of the police, I was not allowed to be involved. I apologize if something so inappropriate was told to you."

Mr. Bouvier, sensing his wife may have crossed the line, apologized, "I'm sorry for what was just said. We have no right to intrude on your personal life."

Charlie added, "No one knows what the person is going through unless they've experienced what you did last night. You were faced with a tremendous loss, and may I say, you handled it all with grace and dignity."

The Bouviers sat silently while they tried to assimilate what Charlie said. "I guess you're right Charlie. No one knew our pain last evening." Mr. Bouvier's eyes filled with tears, and Mrs. Bouvier grabbed a hankie as she dabbed her own eyes.

"Charlie, thank you. I hope you'll forgive us for our mercurial emotions."

"I understand. No hurt feelings. Let me ask you a question, please, Mr. Bouvier. Did you wish to talk to me last evening at 11:15 to go over the details of the event?"

"Oh no, dear," chimed in Mrs. Bouvier. "We told Frederick that if you wanted to go over our final bill last night, that would be fine. That was at 9:30. But he told us you were too busy partying with Simone."

"Well, Mr. and Mrs. Bouvier, let me assure you that at 9:30 I was in the Tavern having dinner, and I would have been more than happy to discuss the details of the evening. I apologize if Frederick let his wild imagination get the best of him. I'll have a talk with him and let him know the inappropriateness of his remarks. He caused you to question our professionalism."

"That is what I said to Mother. You didn't look the type to fool around. I believe you're married, yes?"

Playacting, Charlie answered, "Yes, I am. Separated, actually. The job, you know. It takes all my time and the little woman didn't like me working all these hours."

"Well, we're sorry about that Charlie. Our son, who got married a few years ago is also going through a divorce. He's a very successful attorney and travels a lot. His wife wants him home all the time. So we know what you're going through. Any children?"

"No. No children."

"Well, that's good. Children just complicate the situation." Mr. Bouvier clenched down on his smokeless pipe, the tension visible in his jaw muscles.

"Mr. and Mrs. Bouvier, I will get your final bill together and mail it to you. You don't have to take care of it right now. I believe there is a modest amount due. Please, feel free to review it with your attorney."

"Oh no, Charlie. We want to settle the bill right now," Mr. Bouvier answered.

Charlie produced the bill and Mr. Bouvier wrote out a check for the full amount. He then took out five crisp $100 bills and handed them to Charlie. "This is for you."

"Oh no, Mr. Bouvier, I couldn't accept . . . "

"But we insist, dear," chimed in Mrs. Bouvier.

"Thank you. This is very generous of you."

"Our pleasure, Charlie. We just wish the event had been for Casey's wedding and not her memorial." Mrs. Bouvier began to sob again.

Mr. Bouvier asked, "Do you know if Simone has checked out yet?"

"I don't know, sir. You can check at the front desk. I'm sure Ms. Simpson wouldn't leave without speaking to you first."

Charlie opened the office door, and as he suspected, Frederick was standing there. The Bouviers shook Charlie's hand, and said goodbye to Frederick. Mr. Bouvier placed his hand under his wife's elbow, and guided her towards the lobby.

"A class act after all," Charlie muttered out loud.

When he had called his father yesterday to tell him what had happened, Charlie had suggested giving the Bouviers a discount. After all, not all of the food ordered would be served, and probably the drinking would be cut down as well. The bottles of Dom Perignon weren't going to be popped. That alone saved thousands of dollars. Their pain broke Charlie's heart, and he wanted to reciprocate his condolences.

But his father said, "Absolutely not, Charles. That will give them the idea that we are to blame for their daughter's death. No wonder you don't know how to be successful, you want to give the house away for free. Just like that charity wedding on Thanksgiving. You let that Simpson woman convince you to give the hotel services away for free. You cost this establishment a lot of money. And what happened with that, Charles? The bride died a month later. No, no more free stuff."

Charlie wished he had ignored his father and had given the Bouviers something to show how he felt about their situation. He decided he would send a basket of fruit and flowers to their home on behalf of the Hotel.

Charlie looked at Frederick and said, "I'd like to talk to you for a minute."

Frederick came into Charlie's office and sank down into one of the chairs.

Charlie picked up the phone. "Yes, please ask security to come to my office. No, not an emergency. Just send someone here."

"What's up, Uncle Charlie?" Frederick asked, sounding like a guilty child. "Is there something I can help you with, Uncle Charlie?"

"Yes, Frederick. As a matter of fact, I do need something."

"What's that?"

"I need to fire your ass."

"But you can't do that," he said arrogantly. "My mother owns this hotel."

"No, Frederick. Your mother doesn't own this hotel. Your great grandfather and grandfather own it. And until one of them dies, no one owns the hotel. Meanwhile, I am in charge. And as your boss, I'm firing you."

"On what basis?"

"Let's start with your constant snooping. You always seem to be in the wrong place at the wrong time. Any error or misstep by me is reported directly back to my father. You don't think I know? You walk around here as if you're the one in charge, shouting orders to the kitchen and housekeeping staff, and to the vendors. You told the Bouviers that I was partying with Ms. Simpson. Frederick, why would you tell a client such a thing when you know it isn't true? What benefit would it have? Would it make you look like you're in charge, or a big-mouth wash woman?"

"I saw you two in the bar, and then again in her room."

"You did, did you? And how is that?"

"I knew the scotch that I delivered to her room was for you."

"Did you ask Ms. Simpson if she was going to drink the scotch?"

"No, but I assumed . . ."

"Ah, you assumed. You have a lot to learn, and a lot of growing up to do. Your actions caused considerable disgrace to this hotel. The Bouviers said they asked you if I was available to go over the bill at 9:30, not 11:15. You tried ruining my reputation. You acted irresponsibly and therefore, there are consequences. You'd better hope the Bouviers don't sue us. Their attorney is already involved."

"Gee, Uncle Charlie. I didn't mean any harm. Your father asked me to watch and see what you were doing."

"I'm sure my father told you to watch me so you could learn what it takes to be a general manager, not to be a spy. Frederick, right now I hope to never see you back on this property again, but if your mother fights to get you rehired, you'd better stay clear of me.

A few minutes later, a hotel security guard arrived at Charlie's office.

"Please escort Mr. Frederick Murphy off the property. He no longer works here. See that he turns in all his communication devices."

"Yes, sir."

Charlie slumped back down into his office chair. It isn't even 10 am. What else could possibly happen today, he wondered.

CHAPTER 31

Hilda was home, her feet up on the ottoman while watching her favorite television show, Wheel of Fortune. She didn't give Casey a second thought, other than hoping she would keep throwing up all night. She wanted Casey to have a terrible wedding day. She hated that entitled bitch.

There was a knock at the door.

"Damn it. I just sat down," she muttered to herself. "Who is it?"

She tried looking through the peephole, but her granddaughter had hung a drawing on the front door.

"Grandma," she had said, "put it on your front door. When you come home from work you'll think of me, and smile."

And Grandma Hilda had done just that. But now, she regretted that decision.

"What's her last name?" she heard a male voice whisper.

"Voss. Hilda Voss," was the reply.

Another knock.

"Who is it?" she repeated.

"Hilda Voss. It is the Greenwich Police. We need to talk to you about the Grand Hamilton Hotel."

Hilda opened the door as far as the security chain allowed.

"Yes?"

The officers flashed their badges and ID cards.

"May we come in? We need to talk to you."

Hilda opened the door, and the officers walked past the threshold. She looked up and down the hallway before closing the door behind them.

"What is problem, please?" she asked putting on her Hungarian accent a bit thick.

"May we sit down? And could you shut off your TV?"

Hilda did as requested.

"Can I make you some special Hungarian tea? I make Hungarian Goulash for supper. I make some for you."

"No, no thank you," said Officer McGuire. "Your tea is what we want to talk to you about, Miss Voss."

"Oh?"

"Well, it's about one of the brides you worked for today: Miss Casey Bouvier."

"Yes, Miss Casey," Hilda said with affection, playacting as if she really cared about her. "She make beautiful bride, no? You see her? Beautiful girl. Very much love her husband."

Then, to jump ahead of them, so as to make them believe she wasn't hiding anything, she added in almost a whisper, "I make her special Hungarian tea today to help her make babies tonight." Hilda giggled like a little school girl. She wasn't going to let them have anything on her.

"Well, you see, Miss Voss. . . "

"Please. You call me Hilda."

"Yes, Hilda. Miss Bouvier died today."

"Miss Casey? No." Hilda said in disbelief, her hands gripping her face. She stood up and started pacing the kitchen floor. "When I leave my Casey, she very happy. Beautiful bride. You see her? Beautiful."

The officers watched Hilda pace the length of the kitchen.

"Miss Voss . . . I mean, Hilda. Was Casey feeling okay when you saw her? You were the last person to see her alive."

"Oh my. What happen to my Casey? She really die?" A stream of panic flowed through Hilda.

"Yes, we're afraid so."

Hilda feigned grief. "Well, I don't like gossip. I see pill bottles in Miss Casey's bathroom. I don't know what they are. One start with letter X. That I see. Maybe she take medicine and it not good for her?"

"Maybe," the officer replied. "The room service manager said that someone ordered a pot of hot water and one tea cup for Bridal Suite One."

"Yes, I call and order," Hilda answered.

"Do you still have the tea you gave to Miss Bouvier?"

Hilda walked over to her cupboard and took out a very old tin. She brought it to the table and opened it for the police officers.

"It is Hungarian Chamomile. I give to all my brides."

"The investigating police officers, who took all the items from Miss Bouvier's room, said there wasn't a tea cup in the inventory. Would you know what happened to the tea cup and saucer Hilda?"

Now, Hilda really laid it on thick. "I afraid to tell you. I afraid you send me to jail."

"Don't worry, Hilda. The truth is always the best."

"I show you."

The policemen's soft soled shoes squeaked on the linoleum floor as they followed Hilda into her dining room. In the room was a massive, seven-foot curio with glass doors, filled with delicate teacups and saucers. In front of each cup and saucer was a small white card, noting the name of a hotel, location, date, and name of a bride.

"I collect teacups from all my brides. I have over one hundred cups. Fancy ones. Plain ones. I know it is stealing. I'm sorry. But this is nice way to remember my brides. They all beautiful."

The policemen didn't know what to say. They looked at each other, their silence stifled by the radio static. On the bottom shelf, beginning at the end of a long line, was a delicate rose patterned teacup and saucer. The sign under it read: The Grand Hamilton Hotel, Greenwich, CT. June 20, 2015, Casey Bouvier. The officers walked back into the kitchen. "We'd like to ask you some more questions, and then we'll have to take the teacup, saucer, and the tin of tea to be analyzed."

"Oh no," cried Hilda. "That is all I have of my tea, and I have bride tomorrow."

"I'm sorry Ma'am. As soon as the lab is finished with it, we'll return it to you."

"I'll call my cousin. Maybe she has tea she can give me for tomorrow. Okay. You take and bring back to me."

Hilda had plenty of extra tea stashed in the cupboard. She just wanted to make these cops feel sorry for her.

"How long have you known Miss Bouvier?"

"First time I meet Miss Casey is two months before wedding at hotel. We discuss her makeup and hair, and what she like. Then, I see her again on day of wedding. I work at Hamilton Hotel. Me and five other hair and makeup artists. We take care of all brides, bridesmaids, mommy of bride and mommy of groom."

They asked Hilda for her full name, date of birth, and to see her nationalization papers. They put on rubber gloves and placed the teacup, saucer and tea tin into evidence bags. As they walked back to the police car, one of the officers observed, "Did you notice she didn't ask why we needed to take the tea or the cup?"

"She probably doesn't have anything to hide," answered his partner.

Hilda went into her purse and removed the towel she had used to dry the teacup and saucer in Casey's bathroom. She tossed it into her trashcan. She eyed her tea stash in the small plastic bag. She put the concoction in the cabinet's secret compartment with her collection of teacups, away from curious eyes.

CHAPTER 32

Charlie took two more Advil. His coffee cup was empty, so he had to swallow the pills dry. He picked up the phone, and called his father to tell him that he fired Frederick, and to update him on the end result of the memorial.

"The Bouviers just left my office. It was a very successful transformation, dad. They were very pleased with the outcome."

"I'm happy to hear that, Charles. This incident, although terrible, is a feather in our cap."

Charlie wondered. "How so?"

"Well, it shows we have staff that can take care of last minute emergencies, think creatively, and do a professional job."

"It was Ms. Simpson who came up with the whole idea. At first, I was against it, thinking it was disrespectful and . . . "

"Yes. Yes, you would be against it, Charles. That's because you can't think creatively," his father interrupted, his gruff voice raised.

"Thanks a lot for your vote of confidence, dad."

"Well it's true, Charles. If you were like your sister Harriet, you'd be more successful. She's got a master's degree in economics, and has raised her boys to be aggressive and well-educated. Even your sister Margie has degrees. . ."

This time it was Charlie who cut into the conversation, "Is this a dig that Eve and I never had kids? Or that I didn't get a master's degree? Well, I fired Harriet's kid Frederick this morning."

"You what," his father screamed into the phone, a sound Charlie's head didn't appreciate.

"That's right. I fired Frederick. Little smart-ass Frederick. He walks around here like he owns the place. He told me I couldn't fire him because his mother owns the hotel. He's been nothing but trouble since he was made assistant manager. He bosses people around, talks down to them, and snoops on everything and everyone. He barges into my office without knocking, lingers outside my room, and told the Bouviers that I was acting inappropriately with the wedding planner. He was informing the hotel guests that the bride was killed. Can you imagine our reputation if the guests thought we allowed a killer to walk the halls? You think you've got it on me, dad, but you don't. I'm much smarter than you think."

"I didn't mean it that way, Charles."

"Yes, you did. I'm fed up with your arrogance, making me feel like I'm a child. I left Eve because of her condescending attitude, and the way she likes to spend the Hamilton money. Unfortunately, I'm stuck being related to you."

Charlie opened his desk drawer, poured two TUMS into his mouth and started chewing.

"Okay, Charles. Calm down, before you say anything you'll regret. Let's chalk this all up to the stress relating to the death of the bride." He changed the subject. "Tell me again, why you fired Frederick?"

Charlie's head was pounding, but continued. "The Bouviers offered to pay their bill last evening, but Frederick told them I was partying with Ms. Simpson. When in fact, I was in the Tavern having dinner."

"Well Charles, that's unforgivable. That isn't the kind of image we want for our hotel, is it? No, you were right to tell him to leave."

"I didn't tell him to leave. I fired him."

"Yes, Charles. You fired him. I'll talk to him and see what we can do."

"What do you mean, 'what we can do'? I don't want him back on this property again. If you want to put him at one of the other halls, that's fine. But keep him away from me. I also don't appreciate you undermining my decisions. You put me in charge as General Manager, and whether you like it or not, I'm in charge of this part of the hotel."

"Okay, Charles. Maybe you should take a day off and clear your mind."

"As a matter of fact dad, I'm taking the rest of the week off."

"You can't take that kind of time off now. It's our busiest season," his father shouted into the phone, which didn't help Charlie's hangover.

"You can get someone else to cover during the week," Charlie said. "I'll be back on Friday, in time for that night's wedding."

"I'll come over and take charge. I can't rely on you to do anything right." His father slammed the phone down - a sound Charlie didn't need vibrating in his brain.

Charlie lifted the phone again, and made a call to Simone. "I need to talk to you as soon as possible," he said. "A lot has happened since I left you earlier. Can you meet me for breakfast at Dunkin' Donuts on Greenwich Avenue?"

"Wow, Charlie, this sounds serious," Simone retorted. "I have some phone calls to make, and I want to see the Bouviers before they leave. How about we meet in an hour?"

"Great. And don't tell Jennifer where you're going, please. I assume she's still at Bob's. I'll arrange for a hotel car to take you. Also, call the front desk and ask them for a late check out. I'll see you in an hour."

Simone called her client, Marc Rosenzweig, a private investigator in New Jersey. Simone and Jennifer were the event planners for his son's Bar Mitzvah and his daughter's Bat Mitzvah. Several years later, when his daughter got engaged, Simone and Jennifer were the planners for her engagement party, and then for her bridal shower and the wedding. And a few years after that, his son's wedding.

"Hi Marc. It's Simone Simpson."

"Sim-Sim," he cooed his pet name for her. "How are you? How's Jennifer? Gee, it's great hearing from you."

"Marc, you've always said that if I ever needed your help. . ."

"Don't even ask. What can I do for you?"

"By any chance, do you know the Bouvier family from Summit?"

"No, I don't know them personally, but I heard on the news about their daughter's untimely death.

She filled him in on the events over the past several hours.

"Do you know what she died from? Was it a homicide?"

"I don't know. I doubt the family has gotten back the autopsy report, but I suspect a drug overdose."

Simone continued informing Marc about the pills in the bathroom, how Casey was acting, and that Jennifer had said there was blood on her dress. She also told him about the subsequent memorial.

"How can I help, Simone? It sounds like it could be an easy case if they find it was a drug overdose. Why would you want to investigate her death? Wouldn't the police do that if they thought there was foul play?"

"Well, Marc, there's a few things nagging at me about some of the folks surrounding this bride, and I don't think the police will take it in that direction. Would you be able to check out a few people for me? If my allegations are false, that's great. But, you know my woman's intuition. Please send anything you have to my home address. I don't want anyone in the office knowing what I'm doing. And, of course, include your bill."

Simone gave Marc the names she wanted investigated. "And Marc, only call me on my cell phone, and don't discuss this if you happen to speak to Jennifer."

"First, let me see if I can find anything on these folks. And, as always, everything is confidential. Give me a few days."

"Thanks so much, Marc. Love to Shelly and the kids."

Simone then sent Jennifer a text saying she was going for a long walk, and would be back by noon.

At 11:15 am, Simone arrived at Dunkin' Donuts. Before she walked in, she watched Charlie through the window. He looked awful. There was a large cup of coffee and a half-eaten donut in front of him, plus a yellow-lined note pad. He was staring out to space, clicking his pen.

"Gee Charlie, a night of lovemaking didn't seem to do you any good," she said jokingly, breaking his concentration.

He stood up, gave her a light kiss on the cheek and held the chair for her.

"I fired Frederick," he began.

"Wow. But before you tell me this, I think you lured me here with the promise of breakfast. I'm starving, and I desperately need coffee."

Charlie went to the counter, and returned a short time later with a breakfast sandwich and a large, steaming cup of coffee.

Charlie told her about his conversation with the Bouviers, and that Frederick told them we were partying. "He said he knew the scotch was for me. I didn't deny or confirm."

He continued regaling her with the argumentative conversation with his father, and that he was taking time out for a week's vacation. Simone tried to interject, but Charlie raised his hand to stop her.

"I'm going to enjoy the amenities at The Grand Hamilton Hotel, something I've never done all the years I'm working there. I'm going to get in a game or two of golf, go swimming, play tennis, sit by the pool and read. I'll go to the spa for a massage. I need to figure out what I want to do with my life."

After Charlie's soliloquy, Simone sat back and stared into her coffee. She remained silent.

"It's a lot to take in, Charlie. If you stay at the hotel for a week, it is going to be impossible not to get wrapped up with the everyday routines and problems. How are you going to tell the hotel staff that you can't help them because you're on vacation? Especially now that Frederick is gone and your father will be there, you'll be criticized even more for your actions."

After a few more moments of thinking, she said, "I have an even better idea. Instead, how about you get away from GH and take a real vacation. Come to my house in Westport and spend the week with me. You won't be too far from the hotel in case of an emergency. No one needs to know where you are. My plans have changed since Jen and I aren't going to California, so I can take a week off as well. I'm going to suggest that Jennifer take time off too. Katy and Jonathan can run the office."

Charlie paused for a moment to absorb Simone's suggestion.

"You're unbelievable, Simone. I knew you'd have a better idea. I can use the amenities at the hotel any time. Thank you, my love. I graciously accept."

Charlie's transformation was palpable.

"The change will be good for you and for me," Simone said. "I'll text you my address. Come around 6:00."

"Perfect," he said with adoring eyes.

Simone stared lovingly at Charlie. This time away would be rejuvenating, not only for Charlie, but for Simone too.

A sense of excitement fluttered through her.

CHAPTER 33

Simone returned to the hotel, and called Jennifer.

"Jen, we have to talk."

"Uh-oh. That doesn't sound good." Jennifer was certain Simone was still upset about not telling her the LA wedding was cancelled.

"Nothing bad. Can you come up to my room?"

"I just need to finish packing. I'll be there in a jiff."

When Jennifer arrived, the two women convened to the sitting area of Simone's suite.

"Wow, Simone. You got a much nicer room than I did. You must have connections," Jennifer said with a sly grin. Simone kept her poker face. Jennifer continued, "So what's up?"

"First, I want to apologize for crossing the line yesterday and suggesting that you need to be careful about getting into a relationship with Bob. It was none of my business. I think the stresses of the day were too much for both of us. I was just trying to protect you; I hope you know that. After having dinner with Bob, I can see why you're attracted to him." Simone lied, but wanted to sound empathic and diplomatic.

Jennifer tried speaking, but Simone continued, "I want to let you know that I'm taking the next two weeks off."

Simone had decided on the ride back from meeting Charlie that she would spend this week with him, and then on Saturday fly down to Virginia to visit with the Smiths and spend the July 4th week with them. She wanted to tell them about Charlie.

"I need to recharge, and I think you should do the same. Since next weekend's wedding was canceled and we only have the event in the Hamptons at the end of July, we can both take time off and let Katy and Jonathan run the Hampton event. Unless you want to take the lead, and take Katy or Jonathan with you. It's up to you."

"I never thought I'd hear you say you're taking a vacation. But I can see how vacations would be good for both of us."

Jennifer stalled a moment before continuing. "Simone, you and I don't often discuss our personal relationships, and for good reason, but I want . . . no, I need to talk to someone."

Before Simone could respond, Jennifer started recapping last night's adventure.

"Bob is weird. Very weird. He wanted me to do a three-way with his next door neighbor. I told him I don't do that. Then, he wanted me to do drugs with him and I said no. But he did. I was going to ask him to bring me back to the hotel, but I thought it wasn't a good idea after he had snorted coke. Then he asked me to put on a white garter belt and stockings. I didn't think that was too kinky, and since I had said no to every other thing he wanted, I obliged. But, as I walked out of the bathroom wearing only the garter, stockings and my bra, I remembered where I saw the same sort of lacy garter. When Hilda came back to the room, she had told Casey to go wash her face. Remember that?"

Simone nodded, shocked that Jennifer was sharing these details.

"Casey was wearing the same garter and stockings when she took off her wedding dress."

Simone emitted an audible sound of disgust. "Yes, I remember. I also recall noticing that she had no pubic hair, and how skinny she was."

"Naturally, I couldn't believe the coincidence. It went downhill from there. Simone, he wanted to handcuff me to the bedpost and take photos. I told him I was leaving and he begged me not to go. So, no hand-cuffs, no photos. He promised. Honestly, Simone, I don't know if he took photos of me while I was asleep. I have a feeling he put something in my drink, because I got very sleepy after only one glass of wine. I'm really scared that if he did take photos, he'd put them on the Internet and that could jeopardize your business. And, he didn't want to wear a condom, but again, when I told him I was leaving, he agreed. Simone, even though he's weird and scary, he was an incredible lover."

Simone shifted uncomfortably in her seat, as to where this conversation was headed.

"You know I've been with my fair share of guys, but Bob is different. Maybe it's his bald head, wanting to do unusual stuff, and he's very well hung. I've never been with someone who was so scary and so sexy at the same time. I'm confused. I don't know if I should stay away or be with him."

Simone wanted to pinch herself to be sure she wasn't dreaming this conversation. She forged ahead. "Jennifer, I'm not comfortable talking about this. You and I never discuss our lovers, past or present. And I'd like to keep it that way. You say you're confused. You say he wanted to handcuff you, take nude photos of you, and he possibly drugged you. A second ago you were concerned about my business being ruined. Now, I'm confused." Simone could feel her anger rising at this grown woman, twice divorced, who was acting like a hormone-enraged teenager.

"Yeah, but he's such an exciting lover. I've never done a three-way, or been tied up, and maybe I'm thinking that's sort of . . . different."

"Jennifer, remember what I said to you yesterday. We've known each other a long time, and I've never told you what to do when it comes to your personal life. But, I still say, be very careful."

Simone didn't mention that Charlie was going to spend a week at her place in Westport. She, unlike Jennifer, kept her private life separate from her career.

"Maybe you can spend time with your family on Long Island," Simone suggested. "Think things through. Does Bob know where you live?"

"No, I never told him. But if you remember, he got my name and address from my driver's license. I do like your idea. I'll call my folks and tell them I'm coming for a visit."

"How did you leave it with him this morning?"

"He was asleep when I left. I called a cab and got out of there as soon as I woke up. He drank a whole bottle of Jack Daniels last night, on top of what we drank in the restaurant, so he was sleeping that off by the time I got up."

"And you're confused about wanting to see him again? Jennifer, I think he might have put something more than a relaxant in your drink. I think he slipped in a mind-altering drug. You're usually very level-headed, but for some reason, you're not your usual self. You've been seduced by a dangerous guy."

"I know, I'm ashamed of myself," Jennifer admitted. She paused, reflectively. "I think maybe Casey's death and performing CPR on a dead body was just too much."

"Jennifer, learn from this and move forward. We all make mistakes. It sounds like you applied good judgment and got yourself out of there in time. You'll be fine."

While they waited for Simone's car to be brought to the front entrance, she sent two texts: her address to Charlie. And the name, Robert Hathaway, to Marc Rosenzweig.

She was trying to balance her emotions: anticipating spending time with Charlie, shocked that she invited him, and astonishment over Jennifer's story.

They got into Simone's freshly cleaned Porsche Cayenne SUV, and drove back to Jennifer's apartment in Fairfield. All the way, Jennifer was receiving and sending texts. She assumed Jennifer was texting her parents and arranging her visit.

Simone helped Jennifer unload her luggage, and stayed with her until she packed and was ready to go. She didn't want to leave her alone in case Bob showed up. He sounded unstable. Actually, it was Jennifer who now seemed out of control.

"Please go, Simone. I'm fine. I'm leaving in a few minutes after I call my folks."

"Send me a text when you get there?" Simone asked.

"Yes, mommy," Jennifer said snippily. She quickly added, "Sorry, Simone. If I remember, I'll let you know when I get to my parents."

Simone sat in her car and called her clients in LA, who had canceled next week's wedding. She suddenly noticed a dark blue car driving into the parking lot. It drove slowly around the lot, going up and down the six lanes of cars. The driver stopped at Jennifer's car, paused for a few moments, moved on, and parked in a row behind her. Her call to LA ended as the car's engine shut off, but the person didn't exit the car. The tinted windows prevented Simone from seeing who it was, but she could tell from the small amount of daylight hitting the window, that the driver was wearing a baseball cap.

Simone's mind raced. She thought it was Bob. She wondered if Jennifer wanted her to leave the apartment so she could call him. Or, she thought, were they going off somewhere together. Could Jennifer be that foolish? Could she really be captivated with this bad boy? If so, why had she revealed so much about him? Simone was confused.

Simone noticed Jennifer walking to her car. She put her luggage in the trunk, got in her car, and started the engine. She was sure that Jennifer saw her car parked nearby, but didn't acknowledge her. That was strange.

As Jennifer pulled out of the space, the blue car also followed suit. Simone's sixth sense sent off alarms. She attached her seat belt, and followed the car behind Jennifer's.

Simone dialed Jennifer's cell.

Jennifer answered on the third ring. "I'm driving. I can't talk. I'll call you later."

Simone shouted into the phone, "You're being followed."

But Jennifer had already hung up.

CHAPTER 34

Simone was relieved she had time to pick up food for dinner, and air out the house before Charlie arrived. She was certain he had been eating every meal in the Hamilton dining room, and would appreciate a home-cooked meal.

She had a bottle of Prosecco cooling in the ice bucket, and a bottle of Pinot Noir on the counter, opened, and breathing.

Charlie arrived at 6:15 with a huge bouquet of red roses. She smiled first at him, and then at the bouquet. The flowers reminded her of the time Joe proposed. With her arms filled with roses, she headed to the kitchen with Charlie close behind. She reached up to the top shelf of the cupboard and retrieved a large crystal vase. She opened her utility drawer and removed a pair of floral sheers. He watched as she deftly trimmed the stems and placed the flowers in the vase. While she stepped back to admire her handiwork, Charlie wrapped his arms around her waist. She turned around into his embrace, and he kissed her lips, her face, her nose, and her neck.

"Let me shut off the grill first," she begged, a giggle in her voice. Simone was shocked at herself. She had never been this abandoned with a man before. Not even her husband.

She grabbed a throw blanket from the sofa and covered the ex-pensive Persian rug on the living room floor, their impromptu bed for impulsive lovemaking. The opened French doors welcomed a sea breeze that cooled their bodies during their passionate lovemaking. The only neighbor watching their romp was Long Island Sound.

While Charlie rested, she showered quickly and dressed in a sleeve-less sundress. While she prepared dinner, Charlie showered and got into his well-worn jeans and short sleeve polo short. They were both barefoot. He looked happy, relaxed, and sexy.

Charlie helped Simone set the table on her wooden deck over-looking the Sound. She lit three candles around the centerpiece of fresh flowers, and several others around the deck. The air off the Sound was refreshing, carrying with it a hint of salt water, unlike the stale recycled air at the hotel. She caught herself humming to the soft music coming from her stereo. She stopped, closed her eyes, and took in a deep breath. The late June air dried her damp hair. She was grateful and happy, feelings that had evaded her for such a long time. Maybe something could come out of this relationship, after all.

Charlie opened the bottle of Prosecco, and they toasted to the future week together, away from the hotel.

For appetizers, she prepared grilled, pencil-thin asparagus wrapped in thinly sliced, salty prosciutto, a platter of sliced heirloom tomatoes topped with buttery, silky burrata sprinkled with a chiffonade of fragrant basil leaves, and a circle of oven roasted jumbo shrimp cuddled around a bowl of spicy, home-made cocktail sauce.

The entrée was grilled, tender filet mignon and roasted potatoes. The entrée was complimented by the Pinot Noir.

Keeping with her French upbringing, the meal was followed by a mesclun greens salad, lightly dressed with fruity extra virgin olive oil, freshly squeezed lemon juice, and a hint of spicy Dijon mustard. The platter was topped with a round of tangy goat cheese.

As a grand finale, she presented an assortment of petits fours served with strong and delicious coffee brewed in a French Press.

They had left behind the tragedy of Casey's death, the scramble of turning a wedding into a memorial, and Frederick being fired. Now, Simone had a man living in her home, and sleeping in her bed for a week. What a difference a day makes.

At 9:10 pm her cell phone rang, snapping both of them out of their dreamy state.

"Don't answer it," Charlie begged.

"I have to. It's Jennifer's ringtone."

"Hi. You okay?" she asked Jennifer.

"I'm at my parent's house in Long Island. Things are the same here; my dad and brother are drunk. My dad's health is deteriorating. Thanks for the voice mail about someone following me, but there was no one behind me."

Simone suspected that Jennifer was lying about not being followed, and said, "I'm glad you're okay. I'm with a friend, so I'm going to have to hang up. Have a good week with your folks. Let's touch base over the weekend. Good night."

Simone felt not only annoyed, but suspicious. Something continued to nag at her. An unsettling feeling took hold. As far as she knew, Jennifer never lied to her, but this time, Simone wasn't sure.

She told Charlie what happened, but didn't divulge Jennifer's scary night at Bob's place. That was not Simone's secret to share.

"Okay, enough about Jennifer," Charlie said while raising his glass of wine. "To us."

"To us," Simone replied.

After dinner, they moved from the sundeck to Simone's down-filled white sofa. Charlie stretched his body with his head resting on a back pillow. He looked ten years younger. The stress of the hotel business had vanished. He savored a glass of single malt scotch floating in a Waterford tumbler. He occasionally held the crystal glass up to the light, admiring the rainbow prisms.

Simone sat next to him with her feet underneath her, enjoying the last of the Pinot Noir. They kept their conversation to current events, their respective childhoods, and stayed away from discussing the hotel, Jennifer, weddings, or Casey.

Their week was blissful. They spent it lounging by the pool at Longshore, swimming in the cool waters of Long Island Sound, and one day played a round of golf. They woke up every morning before 5:00 am and took a long walk along Compo Beach, watching the sunrise, looking for sea glass and unusual shells. Following that, they either had breakfast at the Sherwood Diner, or at Oscar's where they sat outside people-watching.

On Thursday, they explored downtown Fairfield. They stopped at The Chef's Table for lunch. Charlie devoured spicy, creamy avocado soup, and Simone enjoyed a bowl of classic gazpacho. Both soups were served with a piece of freshly baked, crunchy bread. The owner, Rich Herzfeld was there and gave Simone a big hug and kiss.

"This is my friend, Charlie. Charlie, Rich."

"Hope you're enjoying your soup."

"Delicious."

"Thanks. Enjoy your lunch. Good to see you again, Simone."

Rich started to walk away, stopped, and turned back, "Simone, I saw your sidekick here yesterday with some guy. A little creepy looking, bald, lots of tats. She didn't introduce me. I hope he's not one of your wealthiest clients," Rich kidded.

"Nah, probably some homeless guy she wanted to feed," Simone responded, the whole time thinking it was probably Bob. She wouldn't be surprised if Bob was at Jennifer's place, and that she never went to Long Island. Maybe Jennifer assumed Simone was in Virginia visiting the Smiths', and they wouldn't run into each other.

Charlie gave Simone a knowing look, "Do you think Jennifer didn't go to her parent's house?" he asked.

"I don't know, Charlie. I just hope she didn't lie to me, when she was really here in town with Bob Hathaway. Maybe she was at her folks' when she called me, only stayed for a day or two, and came back early. I'll talk to her over the weekend. But for now, let's enjoy the rest of our lunch. Then, I'll give you the nickel tour."

While they stood near the crosswalk waiting for the green light, Charlie pulled Simone into his arms and kissed her passionately. "I'm having a wonderful time."

"Me, too."

Holding hands, they crossed, and walked into Fairfield Center Jewelers, Simone's top recommendation to couples looking for an engagement ring, wedding bands or jewelry for any occasion – or, no occasion at all. Simone received a big hug from Bobby Sussman, the owner. He greeted Charlie with a strong handshake.

"Nice to meet you, Charlie," Bobby said. "Here to buy an engagement ring?" he teased while looking at Simone. Apparently, he saw their moment of passion in the crosswalk.

"Oh stop it, Bobby," she laughed. Looking back at Charlie, she joked, "He says that to all the guys I bring in here."

"Oh, really, now?" Charlie quipped, playing along with her game of jealousy.

"I told Charlie all about you, Bobby. He's the General Manager at the Hamilton Hotel in Greenwich, and is often asked for a jeweler recommendation."

"Thanks. You're always thinking of your friends."

"Hey, Simone, take a look at this diamond tennis bracelet," Charlie said.

"Before you say anything, Charlie," she whispered, "thank you, but no thanks."

"Maybe one day," he whispered back.

They drove back to Westport where Charlie was spellbound by Tunnel Vision, a creative, lenticular art exhibit created by Westporter, Miggs Burroughs. The exhibit presented sixteen frames, each one portraying the hands of Westport residents.

Simone and Charlie shopped and explored the town of Westport. From there, they went to a free concert at the Levitt Pavilion, where they danced to a samba band. Then on to a late seating at DaPietro's, a quaint, thirty-seat restaurant, and Simone's favorite in all of Fairfield County. Pietro greeted them personally, and gave Simone a kiss on both cheeks. Simone was Pietro's wedding planner years ago, and he always showered her with kindness.

The feast commenced with crab cakes served over a mesclun salad. Pietro had shared his recipe with Simone, but no matter how many times she made them, the crab cakes were never as delicious as his.

They were then presented with an appetizer of homemade gnocchi, soft pillows of lusciousness covered with homemade pesto sauce and a dusting of sharp, nutty flavored Parmigiano-Reggiano cheese.

For an entrée, Charlie had crispy-skin roasted duck with a wild cherry and calvados sauce. Simone had perfectly seared sea scallops lightly seasoned with Provençale herbs, served with roasted tomatoes and a bed of garden-fresh sautéed spinach.

They ended the meal sharing profiteroles au chocolat, puff pastry with homemade vanilla ice cream, topped with warm Belgian chocolate ganache.

They continued to talk about Charlie's future over cappuccino, followed by complimentary Limoncello.

"I think this past week was a revelation that I can have a life outside of the Hamilton," Charlie said. I still need to do more soul searching, but I don't feel as confused or as overwhelmed as I did . . . was that just four days ago? When I get back, I'll have a heart to heart talk with my father, to discuss my hotel future, and explore going for my MBA. I also need to be more proactive about going ahead with the divorce. Our marriage was over years ago, but I felt obligated to stay with Eve. The guilt was all-consuming."

"By the way, Charlie. Where did you tell your wife you were this week?"

"I didn't. I saw her three weeks ago for dinner. I think she's enjoying her new-found freedom, which is fine with me."

"And your dad?"

"I didn't tell him where I was going, either. I only said I was taking a week off, and would be back in time for Friday night's wedding. If anyone needs me, they have my cell number."

"Charlie, I think you're going to have to roll me home. What a meal."

"That really was incredible. Simone, I wish I could stay with you longer. I wish our time together would never end. I dread having to go back to the hotel tomorrow."

Simone didn't feed into Charlie's desire to continue his stay with her. Nor did she want to feed the folks next to them any gossip.

"Let's go home." Simone surprised herself, as if Charlie lived there as well. What did it all mean, if anything?

"Ciao Ciao, Pietro. Delizioso." Kisses and handshakes were exchanged. "Give my love to Janine and the kids."

Pietro gave Simone a wink and a big smile. "I like this one," he whispered to her. She smiled back, "Me too."

Simone didn't want their magical time together to end. The weather was perfect, the relaxation invigorating, and the lovemaking even better. Simone always thought of herself as a hard woman to break, but it seemed Charlie was able to get through that protective shell.

When they returned to Simone's house, there was a voice message from Marc in New Jersey. "Hi Simone. I overnighted a FedEx envelope to you. You should have it by 10:00 am. Read through it, then get it to the Greenwich Police Department as soon as possible. No need to call me back tonight."

Charlie overheard the message. "What's that about?"

"A hunch I had. I called for reinforcements," she said, being secretive. "I can't say anything now Charlie, but you'll know soon."

As promised, the FedEx envelope arrived on time. While Charlie was in the shower Simone ripped it open, and quickly scanned the material. She called Officer John McGuire, the investigating officer in Casey's death, and made an appointment to meet him at 2:00.

"Sure, Miss Simpson, I'll be here. Just ask for me at the front desk."

At 1:00 pm Simone headed to the Greenwich police station, and Charlie headed back to the hotel.

CHAPTER 35

Officer John McGuire, along with Detective Richard Richardson studied the documents Simone presented them.

"Well, you've been busy, Miss Simpson. What caused you to investigate Miss Bouvier's death further?" asked Detective Richardson.

"Things weren't adding up," Simone replied. "I have an inherent sense when things seem amiss. There were too many questions in my mind, and I couldn't rest until I got some answers. If my suspicions are false, then fine. But obviously, they weren't; they were solid.

"As you can see from the report, and the autopsy, Miss Bouvier's death was not accidental. There were a few items discovered that were quite shocking. I'm happy you've agreed to investigate her death further."

Detective Richardson sent certified letters to people involved with the Bouvier wedding. They were requested to attend a meeting on Tuesday, July 14, 2015 at 10:00 am at The Grand Hamilton Hotel. If they refused to attend, they'd be subpoenaed. The names included:

Bruce and Amanda Bouvier

James and Patricia Michaelson

Patrick Michaelson

Hilda Voss

Robert Hathaway

Frederick H. Murphy

Simone Simpson

Jennifer Keys

Charles Hamilton V

Charles Hamilton VI

As requested, On Tuesday, July 14, The Bouviers and the Michaelsons came with their respective attorneys. Also in attendance was Greenwich Police Officer John McGuire.

"Everyone, please take a seat and we will proceed with our findings," announced Detective Richardson.

"As you know, Miss Casey Bouvier passed away on the day of her wedding at approximately 1:30 pm on June 20, 2015."

Mrs. Bouvier gave out a loud sniffle. "There, there, Mother," whispered Mr. Bouvier.

The detective continued, "The autopsy shows that Miss Bouvier died of a drug overdose. Traces of alcohol, Xanax, Valium, cocaine, heroin and bath salts were found in her blood stream. According to the State Medical Examiner, it was the cocaine cocktail that killed Miss Bouvier."

The sound of Mrs. Bouvier's cries could be heard above his voice. Mrs. Michaelson took out a tissue, too, and wiped her eyes. "I'm so sorry, Amanda," she said. "I truly am."

"We've asked you here today to provide answers to your questions. There will be some upsetting facts revealed, but by the end of this meeting, we will have the person responsible for Casey's death."

"You mean our daughter was murdered?" cried Mr. Bouvier.

"I'm afraid so, sir."

"But that's impossible. Who in this room would want her dead?" With that, Mr. Bouvier turned his head, lifted his hand and pointed at Patrick. "You," he shouted. "You, you killed our little girl."

"Me? I had nothing to do with her death," Patrick hollered.

Detective Richardson cut off Mr. Bouvier. "No, Mr. Bouvier. Patrick had nothing to do with your daughter's death. In fact, he had a lot to gain by marrying your daughter. He would be marrying a wealthy woman who would eventually inherit your money, something Patrick needs desperately right now. You see, Patrick Michaelson has a drug dependency, which has put him into a financial bind."

"What are you talking about, detective?" asked Mr. Michaelson. "Our son has a good job; makes a lot of money. Yes, he had a drug problem, but that was in the past."

This time the detective cut off Mr. Michaelson. "Yes he did have a serious drug problem, and did two stays at rehab centers."

"Oh my," said Mrs. Bouvier. "We had no idea."

"It seems Patrick has gotten himself involved again with drugs, and with someone who is blackmailing him," said the detective.

"Is this true, Patrick?" asked Mr. Michaelson.

"I don't know what he's talking about," Patrick shouted.

"Maybe these photographs will answer your questions." Detective Richardson passed along six photographs of Patrick and Greg kissing outside of Greg's apartment.

"That's disgusting." Mr. Michaelson cringed.

"Oh my, God," Mrs. Michaelson concurred. "That can't be my son."

"Yes, it is your son, Mr. and Mrs. Michaelson. Patrick got involved with this person about six months ago. He's Patrick's supplier, and apparently, Patrick is willing to do whatever he needs to do in order to get drugs. This man has been blackmailing Patrick, threatened to tell Miss Bouvier and you about their relationship."

"What do you have to say for yourself?" asked Mr. Michaelson.

Patrick didn't answer. He just put his head down. Simone could swear she saw a tear roll down his face.

"We'll discuss this when we get home." Then Mr. Michaelson paused for a moment. "You're not arresting our son for Casey's death, are you? You don't think he got the drugs from this . . . this . . . monster, do you?" he said pointing to the photos.

"No, Mr. Michaelson. As I explained, your son didn't kill Miss Bouvier." The detective turned again to their son.

"Patrick Michaelson," the detective said in an amplified tone, "Pay attention." Patrick looked up at the detective. "Mr. Michaelson, you had means and opportunity to kill Miss Bouvier, but no motive.

"Unfortunately, Patrick's addiction costs him about $500 a day. You two," the detective pointed to his parents, "have tried to help him, but can't. You've paid for Patrick's multiple stays in a drug rehab center and you're just about broke trying to save him. You cut him off from your money, but it was a little too late. We believe Patrick was marrying Casey with the hope of getting to her family's fortune."

"Don't say anything," the Michaelson's attorney quickly jumped in.

The same was parroted by the Bouvier's attorney.

"The fact is, Patrick's motive wasn't to kill Casey, but to just get his hands on her money. He would have done anything to protect her. He was looking forward to marrying her so that he could drain another set of parents out of their life savings. No, Mr. Michaelson, your son is not under arrest."

Detective Richardson turned and looked at Hilda.

"Please state your name for the record."

"Hilda."

"Your full name, please."

"Hilda Voss."

"Can you tell us your daughter's name?

She hesitated for a moment before answering, "Florka Bartók."

"Bartók," yelled Mrs. Bouvier.

"Don't say another word," instructed their attorney.

"Can you tell us, how it is you came to be the makeup and hairstylist for Casey Bouvier's wedding?" asked the detective.

"I read in newspaper Miss Casey was getting married. I work many jobs at Grand Hamilton Hotel, so I got luck and got myself hired as one of stylist that day. There are six of us who work here at hotel as independent stylist. When I saw her name on list of upcoming brides, I sign up to work with her." Hilda raised her voice, "She a selfish, conceited person. No one hurt Hilda's family and get away with it."

"Please keep your temper under control, Miss Voss," instructed the Detective.

"I sorry. I want to say that to Miss Casey, but never got the chance. But I can say to her mother and father."

"That's enough, Miss Voss," the detective said as he stopped her from continuing. Mrs. Bouvier sat quietly crying into her handkerchief shaking her head in disbelief, her fingers nervously caressed the pearl necklace.

"Do you know why you were called here today, Miss Voss?"

"No," Hilda said.

"Traces of convallaria were found on the bottom of the teacup the police officers removed from your apartment. It is also known as Lily of the Valley," Detective Richardson explained.

"You killed my baby," shouted Mrs. Bouvier.

"Mr. Reynolds, you must keep your client under control," the detective demanded. He continued, "But no trace of convallaria was found in Casey's bloodstream."

"I don't believe it," mumbled Mrs. Bouvier. Her attorney tapped her arm, and placed his finger against his lips as to say, 'be quiet.'

"Why did you put Lily of the Valley in her tea?" asked the detective.

"Because I want her to suffer like my daughter, Florka suffer every day with pain. She can't have no more babies, her husband leave her. I want to destroy her wedding day, give her rash or stomach ache. I don't want to kill her, just make her remember her wedding day with pain."

"Let me explain," the detective said addressing the others in the room, "Hilda's daughter, Florka Voss Bartók was seriously injured in a car accident by someone driving under the influence."

"She still suffer today," shouted Hilda.

"Please, Miss Voss." He continued, "In the car was her infant daughter who, miraculously, survived the accident. Casey Bouvier was the driver of the car and the Bouvier's settled out of court. They paid Florka Bartók $250,000 to make the case go away."

Mrs. Michaelson whispered to her husband, "That's terrible. I'm glad our Paddy didn't marry into that family."

"I heard that," snapped Mrs. Bouvier, giving Mrs. Michaelson a dirty look.

Detective Richardson turned to Hilda again, "Miss Voss, you had a means, motive and opportunity to commit the crime. We believe you were the last person to see Casey alive."

"I knew it," shouted Mrs. Bouvier.

"Please Amanda," their attorney, Jeremy Reynolds insisted, "don't say anything further. Or the detective will force you to leave the room."

Richardson continued, "Although a trace of convallaria was found at the bottom of the teacup, which was in your possession at your apartment, we cannot prove that you put it there. Someone who had access to the teacup being delivered to her room could have placed it in the cup as well."

The detective turned his attention to, and looked at Frederick.

"Frederick Hamilton Murphy you also had means, motive and opportunity to commit the crime."

"But I didn't do anything," Frederick stammered. "Uncle Charlie, tell them." But Charlie sat quietly, watching his nephew begin to squirm, and enjoying the moment.

"Grandpa, you know I had nothing to do with her death." His grandfather was also silent.

Richardson continued, "I didn't say you did. You knew Miss Bouvier at Princeton, but she never paid any attention to you. You could only admire her from afar. You were the computer major ignored by the popular girls. She was the leader of the pack when it came to bullying you."

"So, that's where I know you," shouted Patrick. "It's been bugging me all weekend. You were the campus geek."

"Patrick, I'd advise you to keep your comments to yourself," said Detective Richardson.

He turned back to Frederick. "You've been snooping around the hotel ever since the Bouvier family arrived. How is it you heard that Miss Bouvier fainted on your walkie talkie? Walkie talkies aren't connected to the hotel's phone system. But you, a computer techie, were able to install a state-of-the-art wireless listening device inside the phone in her room, in your Uncle Charlie's room, and also in Miss Simpson's room. Every time someone used the hotel phone in their room, you heard their conversation.

"You learned about the call for hot water to be delivered to Miss Bouvier's room, and you thought this would be a good opportunity to get Miss Bouvier's attention. Maybe she would recognize you and be pleased to see you. Maybe not. But when you delivered the hot water and teacup to Miss Bouvier's room, she didn't acknowledge you. And this angered you. You also heard that Miss Bouvier had fainted. You ran up to the room and saw Ms. Keys performing CPR on the victim. Because you didn't call your uncle's office from Miss Bouvier's room, gave us a reason to check the phone in that room. That's when we found the listening device. We subsequently checked the other rooms. Since you were fired the morning after the memorial, you didn't have time to return to the rooms and remove the listening devices.

"Why did you leave Miss Keys in the room by herself? Because you knew the communication would have gone right back into your earpiece, and blown your eardrums and your cover. Your motive, unfortunately, was to destroy Mr. Charles Hamilton's reputation because of his affection for Ms. Simpson."

There was silence after Richardson made this announcement. Charlie and Simone avoided eye contact. Jennifer mouthed a, "I knew it," as she exchanged glances with Simone from across the room.

"Is this true, Charles?" Charlie's father said sternly. Charlie avoided eye contact with his father, and refused to answer his accusatory question.

Richardson addressed Frederick again, "You wanted his job, but it doesn't seem to have turned out the way you thought. Everything Mr. Hamilton did, you reported back to his father, your grandfather. You didn't expect Mr. Hamilton to fire you, did you? You thought you had the goods on him. That's a discussion for another time. We don't believe you were the one who killed her."

"I didn't kill her. I swear," Frederick said. "I only delivered breakfast and the tea cup to her room. I never touched the cup, or put anything in it. If I did, Miss Hilda would have seen the poison in the bottom of the cup."

"That's a very good point, Frederick."

"Miss Voss," the detective turned back to Hilda. "Did you see anything at the bottom of the cup before you poured your tea into it?"

Hilda stalled for a moment. She looked over at the detective, then to Frederick, and back to the detective. She could say she saw something on the bottom of the cup and frame Frederick for the crime, but she'd never work at the Hamilton Hotel ever again.

She decided to tell the truth. "No, I see nothing in cup. It was empty. Frederick good boy. He mean no harm."

Charlie looked at Simone who looked like a strutting peacock. "You're a very good sleuth, Ms. Simpson," he whispered with a twinkle in his eye.

"We'll talk later," she whispered back with a schoolgirl grin on her face. "I'm loving this."

"Finally, we come to you, Security Officer Robert Hathaway," Detective Richardson said, turning to Bob.

"Yes?" he responded.

A feeling of anxiety started to infiltrate Jennifer's body. She was sorry she took the seat next to Bob. Jennifer looked directly at Simone and mouthed, "You know something." Simone just nodded her head. Jennifer often commented that Simone has a sixth sense, something which frightened her. "You're a freak of nature." Jennifer often joked.

"Officer Robert Hathaway, like Frederick, you knew Miss Bouvier at Princeton. Did you know Frederick and Patrick while in college?"

"Yeah, I knew them. Frederick was the pimply-faced nerd with a pocket protector and tons of pens. Patrick was the party-boy at the frat house, always stoned. I didn't hang with them, but I knew who they were."

"Were you surprised to see Frederick working here?"

"I knew he was related to the Hamilton family, but I didn't think it was this Hamilton family. It doesn't matter, I have no dealings with him."

"Were you surprised to see the Bouvier and Michaelson wedding being held here?"

"Nah, lots of rich folks have their wedding here," he said with a nonchalant air.

Richardson continued, "You, the popular quarterback, and Miss Bouvier, head of the cheerleaders, were king and queen of the campus. You were attending Princeton on a sports scholarship, with promises of going to the NFL. Is that correct?"

"Yeah."

"You and Miss Bouvier were secretly engaged. Is that correct?"

"Yeah."

"What did he say?" yelled Mr. Bouvier. Only to be silenced by his attorney.

"During the Home Coming game, you were seriously injured during a tackle that left you with a broken collarbone and a serious brain injury. You lost your scholarship at Princeton, your NFL dreams, and Miss Bouvier. You were no longer the successful jock Casey wanted, so she broke off your engagement. Conveniently enough, Patrick came along."

Mr. Bouvier removed his unlit pipe from his mouth, "I can't believe you're saying all this about our daughter, Detective Richardson. We never met this Hathaway fellow. Where are you coming up with all this information?" He turned to his attorney, "Can we sue him for slander?" He replaced the pipe, and nestled it back in the corner of his mouth.

"Let me continue, Mr. Bouvier," said the detective.

Richardson turned his eyes to Hathaway. "Miss Bouvier broke up with you a few years ago, but you still held a grudge."

Hathaway stood and snapped, "Yeah, I was angry. Real angry. That bitch dumped me as soon as I was injured. I had her initials put on my arm as a constant reminder of how she broke my heart." He rolled up his sleeve to show everyone the tattooed, CAB.

Mrs. Bouvier pushed up her eyeglasses to get a better view of the artwork. She wrinkled her nose when she saw the snake entwined in the Rosary beads along with her daughter's initials.

Hathaway hadn't lost a loved one by a cab, it was Casey-Ann Bouvier he had lost, Simone concluded.

"I was very angry. She dumped me because I lost my contract with the NFL. The money wasn't going to be there. She didn't tell you about me," his head nodding towards her parents, "because she was embarrassed. She said she wanted to wait until I signed with the NFL before bringing me home to meet you guys. But I didn't kill her. You have no proof."

Richardson spoke again, "You, like Frederick, have a master key to all the hotel rooms. No one would ever question a Hamilton security guard walking around the hallways of the hotel. Once Hilda left Miss Bouvier's room, you took the opportunity to enter her room and provide her with the lethal dose of drugs. You knew how much she loved cocaine."

Mr. Bouvier removed his pipe to speak, but his attorney, Jeremy, tapped him on the arm, and shook his head as to say, 'be quiet; don't say anything.'

"You're crazy," shouted Hathaway. "I wasn't anywhere near her room. You can't prove it."

"Well, actually we do have proof. We have your fingerprints on the ribbon and the black box found in her room."

"That's because I picked them up from the floor. Ask your cop photographer. He yelled at me for picking it up because I didn't have gloves on."

"You picked up those items on purpose, in case we found your prints on them. But we also found your fingerprints on her dressing table, and dirt in the fibers of the carpet that match the dirt in the security office."

"That still doesn't prove anything," he retorted. "You said it yourself, I picked up the box and the ribbon and placed them on the table. That would put my fingerprints there. As for the fibers in the carpet, yeah, I was in the room. So, that doesn't prove anything."

"We are sure we may find your DNA on her body as well." Richardson planted this fact to see if Hathaway would react.

Hathaway had forgotten he kissed her neck, but sidestepped that fact.

Richardson countered, "In addition, what you all don't know, is that the hotel recently installed surveillance cameras in the hallways. Only Mr. Hamilton knew about the cameras."

"Charles, is this true?" his father asked annoyed. "Who authorized you to spend the hotel's money to install cameras? I certainly didn't."

"Yes, dad. It's true," Charlie answered, confidently. "We've had numerous petty thefts in recent months, and we needed to find the culprit. I kept it a secret from you because I knew Frederick was snooping around and reporting everything back to you. And you would tell him about the cameras. I had the cameras installed on Frederick's days off. The security company worked every Monday and Tuesday until the whole hotel was covered. Anyone who asked what the workers were doing, were told the sprinkler system was being updated. Frederick also doesn't know how to keep his mouth shut. He would have blabbed to the staff, because he knew something they didn't."

"That's not true," snapped Frederick.

Charlie continued, looking at Frederick, "May I remind you that you were telling the hotel guests that the bride was killed? You could have caused a major exodus of our guests. There were other instances, not to be discussed now."

Charlie continued, "I figured, anyone who has access to the rooms, including Frederick, housekeeping, security, and hotel staff, did not need to know about the cameras, until we found out who was stealing from the guests. We caught the suspects, and they were charged and terminated. There is a lot to learn from watching those cameras. In addition, we upgraded our entry system for all the hotel rooms. Now, when someone enters a room, it is electronically recorded. That is why the staff received new passkeys."

Richardson spoke again, "So you see, Officer Hathaway, you were recorded on the cameras entering Miss Bouvier's room, and your passkey was also electronically registered. Your entry to her room matches her time of death. You had means, motive and opportunity."

"And why would I want to kill her?"

"I explained that to you already." Richardson ordered, "Officer McGuire, place Robert Hathaway under arrest."

In a flash, Hathaway was on his feet with his arm around Jennifer's neck. He yanked her out of her chair. He had carefully tucked his off duty gun into his waistband, away from everyone's eyes. Just as swiftly as he got Jennifer in his grip, he pulled out his gun and placed it against her temple. Screams and cries reverberated from everyone in the room. Officer McGuire stepped forward toward Bob.

"Get away from me, or I'll kill her."

Jennifer gave out a muffled scream for help as she clawed at his arms. Detective Richardson and Officer McGuire pulled out their weapons and aimed them directly at Bob Hathaway. "Put down your guns, or I'll shoot her," Bob demanded. "I'll do it." His eyes wide with fury, and a pulsating vein running from his cheek to his bald head, enhanced his looks of a snake.

Officer McGuire looked at Detective Richardson, who nodded to lower his weapon onto the conference room table. He did as ordered.

Hathaway began to drag Jennifer towards the door. Everyone knew he wasn't going to get far; he knew it too. But at least he had a hostage until he could figure out his next plan of action.

Like a frightened child, the scream of, "I'm getting out of here," was echoed by Frederick, sitting closest to the door. He jumped up, opened the door and made a run for it. Hathaway moved his arm away from Jennifer's head and shot at Frederick just as he was on the other side of the door. The sound of the blast caused another round of screaming. Frederick went down in a heap, landing just outside the door. "I'm hit. I'm hit." Cries from Frederick filled the room.

"No one move." shouted Hathaway. "I mean it. I'll kill her if anyone else tries to leave."

Charlie grabbed Simone and pushed her behind him. The husbands did the same with their wives. Cries to stop were aimed at Hathaway.

"Shut up. All of you," shouted Hathaway.

Patrick sat with his head bent, keeping still, oblivious of what was going on. Or, too stoned to realize the danger that surrounded him.

Simone moved from behind Charlie, and looked directly at Jennifer. Simone suddenly began to sing the song, Michelle by Paul McCartney, "Michelle, ma belle."

"What are you doing?" Hathaway screamed.

"I'm singing," Simone answered.

"Simone," Charlie whispered. "Be quiet."

"I sing when I get nervous." She emphasized the word, sing. I'm French, and that is what we do. "I will say the only words I know that you'll understand."

"Well, stop it," Hathaway screamed even louder.

Jennifer and Simone's eyes locked in recognition. Jennifer might be a slim, petite woman, who didn't have good judgment when it came to men, but like Simone, if necessary, she could become a Pit bull. She felt for Bob's foot with her shoe. Bob was yelling at Simone to keep quiet. He then told Richardson, "I want a car to the airport, and a plane." He again pointed his gun at Simone.

At the very second Bob moved his gun away from Jennifer's head and pointed it at Simone, she nodded to Jennifer.

With as much force as possible, Jennifer bashed her elbow into Bob's solar plexus. Then she slammed her expensive spike heel into his instep. He gave out a scream. He shot at Simone, missing her by inches. But the shock of Jennifer's quick actions loosened his grip on her. She whipped around and, with all her strength, pounded the heel of her hand into his nose, and then quickly kicked him in the groin. Hathaway went down in a heap, still holding on to his gun with one hand, and his groin with the other.

Jennifer ran to Simone, and Richardson and McGuire rushed in.

"Put down your weapon," shouted the officers. They picked up their pistols, and pointed them directly at Bob Hathaway.

Meanwhile, Hilda ran from the room to the front desk to call for help. She stopped to check Frederick. He was shot in the leg, whimpering.

The Bouviers and their attorney left the room. Their attorney helped Frederick get out of the doorway, and off to a safer location. The Michaelsons were trying to get their son out, but Patrick just sat, transfixed in the chair. The three of them, and their attorney were trapped in the corner.

"Drop your weapon," the detective shouted at Bob. "Drop your weapon, now," he repeated.

Blood poured from Bob's nose. "You bitch," he spat at Jennifer, blood spewing with his words, landing on the conference room table and onto the rug.

"Let go of your weapon," commanded Officer McGuire. They knew if they tried to shoot him, they might miss and get one of the Michaelsons' standing within inches of Hathaway.

Actions happened at record speed. The police retrieved their guns. Bob raised his shaking hand, holding the gun, while his other hand cupped his groin, now throbbing in pain. Screams were heard again. Charlie, his father, Simone and Jennifer were stuck in a corner of the room, away from the door.

"Get under the table," commanded Charlie. The four of them dropped to their knees – a difficult feat for his father – and they crawled under the table just as a bullet passed Simone's head.

Hathaway turned the gun, and placed it in his mouth. "No! Don't do it. Put the gun down now," Richardson commanded.

Click. The gun misfired.

From under the table, the four could see Richardson and McGuire's feet rushing Hathaway. They tackled him to the ground, and handcuffed him. Simone's and Hathaway's eyes locked under the table. "You bitch. I should have shot you when I had the chance."

The two officers lifted up Hathaway. He was spitting blood and uttering venomous words.

Charlie helped his father crawl out from under the table. Simone and Jennifer stood up, and fell into each other's arms.

"And you," Hathaway said, looking at Jennifer "Casey looked a lot better than you did in those damn stockings and garter."

Sirens could be heard in the distance. It was obvious the hotel staff had been trained to act accordingly in case of any emergency. They quickly cleared the lobby, ushering guests into the Tavern, where the doors were closed and curtains drawn. Valets redirected cars to make way for additional police and emergency vehicles.

You were magnificent, Jennifer," Simone said with complete adoration. "It's over."

"You were the one that was magnificent. It was your singing that jogged my memory and brought back our training."

"Why were you singing, Simone?" Charlie's father asked her.

"Because Jennifer and I were trained in SING, a form of self-defense. When you're around as many drunks as we are, sometimes you need to defend yourself. I believe this is the first time we've ever had to use SING outside the classroom."

"I hope I never have to use it again. You see, Simone, I knew my shoes would come in handy one day." The two women laughed, hugging each other even tighter.

"So what does SING stand for?" asked Charlie.

"S for solar plexus; I for instep, N for nose, and G for groin.

"Well, you were not only brilliant, you were also brave," Charlie said, giving Jennifer a hug. "I thought Simone was strong, but you took Hathaway down in seconds. I'm very impressed . . . and a bit scared," he teased.

Charlie put his arm around Simone and kissed her lightly on the lips. He looked into her eyes and said, "I love you." He didn't care who approved or disapproved, even his father.

His father boomed, "Yes, you were incredible, Jennifer. You too, Simone. In fact, I'd like for you women to consider working here as our in-house wedding planners."

Simone, Jennifer and Charlie laughed aloud.

"I've been trying to get these two to work here for years," said Charlie.

"I see where your son gets his brains, Mr. Hamilton," said Simone.

CHAPTER 36

Robert Hathaway was arrested, and taken away in a police car. He was charged with first degree murder, attempted murder, drug possession, resisting arrest, and unlawfully firing a weapon. Frederick was brought to Greenwich Hospital, where he was treated for a bullet wound to his leg. The Bouviers, and the Michaelsons, and their attorneys returned to New Jersey, with a growing dislike for each other's family. Hilda begged Charles Hamilton V to allow her to continue working at the Hamilton Hotel. He said he would take her request under consideration.

"I have a great idea," Charlie's father said. "How about we get lunch at the Tavern. It's on me."

Charlie squeezed Simone's hand, and whispered, "He's a big shot. He wouldn't be charged for the food, anyway."

"Regardless, it's sweet. I think he wants to get to know Jennifer and me better. Who knows, we might be your boss one day soon," she teased.

The four of them indulged in a delicious celebratory luncheon.

"So Charles," Charlie's father said with a stern voice, "how long have you and Simone been involved? You know, you are still married."

Charlie wanted to burst into a rant. But he held his tongue. Was his father reprimanding him, or informing Simone that he was married? A little of both, thought Charlie. "Well, dad, first of all, Eve and I are officially separated. Simone and I have been involved for several months."

"What?" Jennifer said, shocked. "You're good at keeping a secret, Simone."

"I've had many secrets during my life, Jennifer," Simone said meekly. "This one was more difficult, especially from you. I'm sorry I couldn't say anything, but I'm sure you understand. And, I would appreciate you not saying anything to Katy and Jonathan, or anyone else in the office."

"Dad," Charlie interjected. "Eve and I are in the final stages of our divorce, and I would appreciate if you didn't say anything to anyone else in the family about Simone and me. I'm sure Frederick will tell Eve, and she'll be vindictive and delay the divorce proceedings."

"I won't say a word, son, and I'll tell Frederick to keep his mouth shut as well." That was probably the first time in Charlie's life that his father called him 'son' in a kind and loving way.

After lunch Jennifer went back to the office, and updated Katy, Jonathan and the rest of her staff on the day's unfolding events. Katy said, "I never thought one of us would have to use our SING training. I'm glad it was you, and not me," she added, imagining how frightening the situation must have been.

Charlie returned to Simone's house in Westport. They decided to take the rest of the day off, stroll Compo Beach, and later that evening have dinner at the Whelk.

They made love, committing their affection for each other. Simone snuggled in Charlie's arms afterward, reveling in the fact that Charlie loved her. She mentally flashbacked to her childhood filled with abuse and bullying. She lamented the death of her parents, and the sadness over her relationship with her brother Jean-Paul. A tear streamed down her face and onto Charlie's bare chest, when she thought about how violently Joe had been killed, coupled with the devastating loss of their baby.

Yet, she had survived it all with strength and determination. The road she had traveled was filled with unexpected turns. She reflected on the Smith family, and their involvement in her life . . . their love, devotion and belief in her had helped Simone become the woman she was today.

She thought about having to leave tomorrow for St. Louis, for another high-tension wedding. She didn't want to leave Charlie, but she knew she had to get back to work, and back to her life. Where will their relationship go from here, now that they've proclaimed their involvement to everyone? She pondered that thought as she lay next to him.

Charlie's love warmed her, allowed her to be free to love in return. The protective shield she had built around her was gone. No matter what happens in the future, she would survive.

She suddenly heard two simultaneous pings from incoming text messages. She slipped out of bed, and picked up her cell phone:

"Jonathan took a message from woman in NYC,

wants wedding in Paris. We can call her next week.

I have St. Louis file packed for our trip tomorrow.

Will see you on airport shuttle in the morning. Jen"

Simone texted back: "Thanks. See you on the bus."

She hesitated for a moment before reading the next text. The number was unfamiliar. She paused, and then tapped the message icon:

"I miss you, Simone.

Your one and only true love, Joe."

To be continued...

Coming Soon...

See Paris Before "I Do"

A Simone Simpson Mystery

Spring 2019

www.ingramcontent.com/pod-product-compliance
Lightning Source LLC
Chambersburg PA
CBHW071910220626

47052CB00002B/296